The Ultimate Con

The Ultimate Con

BY

TRACY WILSON

http://beautifulpublications.com

Published by
Beautiful Publications LLC
Stratford, CT 06614

This book is a work of fiction. Names, characters, places, and incidents are either products of the author's imagination or are used fictitiously. Any resemblance to actual events or locales or persons, living or dead, is entirely coincidental.

PRINT ISBN: 978-1-7362753-2-0
EBOOK ISBN: 978-1-7362753-3-7

Printed in the United States of America

Dedication

This 1st series of 2021 is dedicated to my friends Snow & Flick. Thank you for agreeing to be written into my world.

CHAPTER ONE

"Please..." Snow whispered as tears streamed down her face... "I'm begging you... don't make me do this..." Flick sat down beside her, took her face in his hands, and wiped her tears. Snow was trembling as she continued crying and Flick kissed her gently...

"Baby..." he breathed... "Listen to me..."

"Ooo... okay..." Snow sniffed...

"You're my wife..." he breathed as he kissed her...

"I know..."

"You're beautiful..." he breathed as he kissed her again... "And this right here..." he breathed as he put his hand between her legs... "Is all mine..."

"But..."

"Look at me..." he said as he tilted her head up and looked in her tear-soaked eyes... "Do you really think I'ma let another man hurt you?"

"Noo..." she whispered... "But..."

"But what?" he breathed as he began kissing her down her neck...

"What if you don't get there in time?"

"I'll be there from start to finish..." he whispered in her ear as he moved his hands up and down her back...

"You'll be there?"

"Hell yea..."

"What if he wants you to leave?"

"I'll tell him I like to watch..."

"What if he says you can't watch us?"

"If I can't watch..." he breathed as he kissed her again... "Then it's not goin' down..."

"You promise?"

"Once he drinks the champagne... he's ours to do with as we please..."

"What if he won't drink the champagne?"

"Once he sees you in this right here... he'll do whatever you ask..." Flick said as he ran his hand across her breast...

"I'm not sure I can do this Flick..."

"Remember what you did to me?"

"That was different..."

"This is the same thing..."

"What if he wants to fuck right away?"

2

"You tell him what's your hurry... we have all night... and then you pour him another drink..."

"What if he refuses? What if he says he can't wait and he tries to take me?"

"You'll be right over here by the chaise lounge – if he says he can't wait and he wants you right now, then you push him down on his back, I'll cuff his wrists, and before he can object – you climb on top of him, you start rubbing on him, grinding on him, and keep his attention until he passes out..."

"What if he doesn't wake up?"

"He'll wake up..."

"You don't know that Flick..."

"Didn't I wake up?"

"Yea... you did..."

"He'll wake up too..."

"What if he goes to the police?"

"If he goes to the police, he's gonna have to tell them he offered me money to let him fuck my wife..."

"What if the police believe him?" Flick got up, took the micro-recorder out his pocket, and played it back for Snow...

"You have a beautiful wife..."

"Thank you..."

"I'd give anything to spend a night in the arms of a woman as beautiful as she is..."

"Anything?"

3

"I don't understand..."

"My wife and I have always fantasized about having threesomes..."

"I'm not interested..."

"Not me... my wife..."

"Are you saying you'd indulge me?"

"Depends on what you're willing to do..."

"What's it going to cost me?"

"A few hours...under one condition..."

"What's the condition?"

"I get to watch..."

"I don't know if I can do that..."

"I guess you're not willing to do anything..."

"Wait..."

"Yes?"

"I'll do it..."

"You understand I'm watching..."

"As long as that's all you do... I'll see you later tonight..."

"What time?"

"8 pm..."

"Oh shit! I can't believe you recorded that?"

"Hell yea!" Flick exclaimed as they heard a knock on the door..."

"Oh shit – that's him – you ready?"

"I'm ready..."

"Aiight – le'me drop this melatonin in the champagne right quick..." Flick said as he took the melatonin out his pocket, dropped two pills in the champagne, stirred it, and motioned for Snow to open the door...

"Hey..." Snow said as she opened the door wearing a black bustier and black thong panties...

"Hey..." Sean said breathed as he looked her up and down... "May I come in?"

"Of course..." she said as she opened the door wider and he followed her into the room. Snow walked slowly and deliberately, giving him plenty of time to watch the roses and vines tattooed across her ass sway beneath the top of the thong between her cheeks...

"Did it hurt?" Sean asked...

"Did what hurt?" Snow asked as she turned to face him with her hands on her hips...

"This..." he said as he walked up to her and palmed her ass...

"Oooh!" she exclaimed...

"Well... did it?" he asked again as he began massaging her ass...

"No... it's henna...."

"I see... is this also henna?" he breathed in her ear as he ran his hand up her arm...

"Yes... yes it is..." she breathed as she deliberately flung her hair and tilted her head back so he could see her voluptuous breasts peeking over the top of the bustier...

"May I?" he asked as he reached out to touch her breast..."

5

"Please..." she breathed. Flick was giving her the side eye, wondering if she was acting or if she was actually enjoying what was happening...

"Let's have some champagne..." Flick interrupted, picking up a glass for himself and handing a glass to Sean...

"Have a drink with me..." Sean said as he handed a glass of champagne to Snow...

"To all of us..." Snow said as she took a sip...

"To all of us..." Flick said as he took a sip. Sean looked at Flick, he looked back at Snow, and then he hesitated...

"Finish your champagne..." Snow said as she stood in front of him and began rubbing his dick through his pants. That was the turning point for him – he gulped his champagne down, grabbed Snow around her waist, and kissed her hard. Snow was startled when he started to walk her backwards towards the bed but then she remembered what Flick told her... "Let's get on the chaise lounge..." she breathed...

"Let's not..."

"I want to ride your dick and watch you play with my breasts..." she said as she took her breasts out of the bustier and held them up...

"Fine..." he said as he went over to the chaise lounge and lay back...

"That's what I'm talkin' about..." she said as she straddled him and began grinding on him...

6

"Come here..." he growled as he sat up, held her, and began sucking her breasts... and then he fell back against the chaise lounge...

"Oh shit! He's dead!"

"He's not dead..." Flick said as he went over to him and checked for a pulse...

"Can I get up now?"

"Yea Baby – take his wallet out his pants..." Flick said as he cuffed his wrists to the chaise lounge and then he took Sean's cell phone out his pocket...

"Why are you cuffing him?"

"I'm cuffing him so he doesn't fall on the floor – turn on the computer..."

"Okay!" Snow exclaimed as she turned it on...

"Take out his driver's license..."

"Okay..."

"What kinda credit cards does he have in his wallet?"

"He has American Express, MasterCard, Visa... and a Debit card...

"Le'me see those..." Flick said as he looked at the cards... "Okay – this whatchu do..."

"What?"

"Go to the Bank of America..."

"Okay..."

"Type in Capital Holdings as the user name...

"Okay..."

"Click on the forgot password link..."

"Okay..."

"Now I wait for the email confirmation... now I just reset his password... now I confirm it... and now I delete these from his phone and his email... okay – type in Myholdings1 as the password – capital M..."

"Okay... I'm in..."

"Click on another tab..."

"Okay..."

"Log into our other account..."

"Not the main one?"

"No – the one we have with Webster..."

"Okay... I'm in..."

"Good – how much money does he have in his account?"

"Oh shit – Flick – he has $50 thousand dollars in this account!" she whispered...

"Good – transfer $45 thousand dollars to our account..."

"Okay!" Snow exclaimed as she typed in the information, hit the buttons, and executed the transfer... "Done!"

"Okay – log off the computer..." he said as Sean's cell phone rang...

"Hello?"

"Mr. Stewart this is Bank of America..."

"How can I help you?"

"We see that you just transferred $45 thousand dollars into an account at Webster Bank..."

8

"Yes Maam – I'm adding another property to my portfolio..."

"Thank you for verifying the transfer Mr. Stewart – have a good night..."

"You too..." Flick said as he hung up the cell phone and then picked up the desk phone...

"Front desk..."

"Yes – could you send security up to my room please?"

"Is there a problem?"

"We invited Mr. Stewart to our room for drinks and he's passed out drunk..."

"Oh my..."

"I'd help him back to his room but I don't know what room he's in..."

"Okay – we'll send somebody right up..."

"Flick – what are you doing?" Snow whispered...

"I asked for security to come up – I'm going to help security get Mr. Stewart back to his room..."

"What if he wakes up?"

"So what – I'll tell him we had a great time and he needs to go sleep it off..." Flick explained as security knocked on the door... "Hang on!" Flick said as he uncuffed him and put Sean's cell phone back in his pocket. Snow hurried into the bathroom and Flick let security in...

"He had too much to drink huh?"

"Yea man..." Flick laughed...

9

"C'mon – you get one side –I'll get the other side... security said as they both lifted Sean up...

"C'mon Mr. Stewart – let's go..." security said as they drug him out the room. Snow hurried out the bathroom and then she saw it...

"Shit! His wallet!" Snow grabbed the wallet, threw on a robe, grabbed the room key, and ran out the room and down the hall... "Flick!"

"Snow – what's wrong?"

"His wallet..." she panted as she handed it to security...

"Thanks..." security said as they got him to his room and Snow ran back to their room...

"Oh shit – we don't have his key...' Flick said...

"Don't worry – I have a pass key..." security said as they got Sean into his room...

"Time to go night night..." Flick said as they put him on his bed...

"Thanks for your help..." security said...

"Thank you..." Flick said as they left Sean's room...

"If you need anything else – just call..." security said as he went to the elevator, got in, and went downstairs as Flick went back to their room...

"We good?" Snow asked...

"We good..." Flick smiled... but we gotta check out..."

"We gotta check out now?"

"We have to – we don't want to be here when he wakes up..."

"Okay..." Snow sighed... "Le'me throw this shit in the duffel bag...

CHAPTER TWO

"Oh God..." Sean moaned as he slid out the bed and dragged himself to the bathroom. Sean made it to the bathroom just in time... "Uggh! Uggh! Uggh!" he groaned as he heaved over the toilet... "What the fuck happened to me last night..." he moaned as he flushed the toilet and turned to look at himself in the mirror... "I look like shit!" he exclaimed when he saw how disheveled he looked. Sean reached for the mouthwash, opened it, poured the entire bottle into his mouth, swished it around, and spit it out into the sink... "Still look like shit..." he said as he opened the toothpaste, put some on the toothbrush, and proceeded to brush his teeth... "Hold on..." he said as he heard a knock on his room door. Sean went out into the bedroom towards the door, looked out the peephole, and saw security... "Who is it?"

"Security..."

"How can I help you?"

"Can I come in?"

"Sure..." Sean answered as he opened the door... "What seems to be the problem?"

"I just came to see how you were doing..."

"How I'm doing? I don't understand..."

"You don't remember what happened last night?"

"I don't remember anything about last night..."

"You were pretty drunk..."

"Really? I don't remember drinking..."

"Mr. Alexander called us to come help get you back to your room..."

"Mr. Alexander?"

"Flick and his wife..."

"Ooohhh... I see..." Sean said as he began to remember...

"You had one too many, you passed out, and Mr. Alexader couldn't get you back to your room so he called us..."

"Oh my God – if I did anything stupid – I apologize..."

"Naaa... you weren't any trouble – we brought you in here, put you in bed, and you went to sleep as soon as you touched down..."

"Good lookin' – thanks..."

"You're welcome..."

"What room is Flick in – I wanna go thank him too..."

"They checked out early this morning..."

"Oh shoot – that's too bad..."

"Well – I just wanted to make sure you were okay – I'm on my way home..."

"Okay – thanks..." Sean said as he opened the door and security left... "Now I'm gonna get me a shower, get dressed, get some breakfast, and dream of Snow..." he said as he stripped out of his clothes, walked into the bathroom, turned on the shower, and got in... "I wish Snow was here now..." he whispered as he stood under the water and began stroking his dick... "Mmmm... Mmmm... Mmmm..." he moaned as he began to remember the way her ass swayed back and forth... "Mmmph... Mmmph... Mmmph..." he moaned as he remembered palming her ass... "Mmmph... Mmmph... Mmmph..." he moaned as he remembered her pushing him down on the chaise lounge... "Mmmph... Mmmph... Mmmph..." he moaned as he remembered kissing her breasts... "MMMPH... MMMPH... MMMPH..." he moaned as he imagined her riding his dick... "UUUGH!   UUUGH!   UUUGH! FFFUUUCCCKKKK!" he moaned as he came all over himself... "To bad you checked out early..." he panted as he began washing himself... "I would've been willing to do anything for another night..." he sighed. After he finished taking his shower, he got out the tub, shaved, and went into the bedroom to get out fresh clothes... "Hmmm..." he said as he looked at his cell phone... "Why is the Bank of America calling me?" he asked as he answered... "Good morning – this is Sean..."

"Mr. Stewart, this is Bank of America Customer Service..."

"Is everything alright?"

"Everything's fine – we're just calling to let you know your transfer is complete..."

"Transfer? What Transfer?'

"You transferred $45,000 to an account at Webster Bank..."

"I didn't transfer any money last night!" Sean snapped...

"Mr. Steward – I apologize for any confusion – according to our records, you requested a new password, you logged into your account, you made the transfer, and when we called you, you verified there was no fraudulent activity on your account..."

"Your conversations are recorded – right?"

"Yes sir..."

"Could you play the conversation back for me?"

"Yes sir – hold on..." Sean's nostrils flared and his chest heaved as he heard Flick's voice...

"Hello?"

"Mr. Stewart this is Bank of America..."

"How can I help you?"

"We see that you just transferred $45 thousand dollars into an account at Webster Bank..."

"Yes Maam – I'm adding another property to my portfolio..."

"Thank you for verifying the transfer Mr. Stewart – have a good night..."

"You too..."

"Are you still there Mr. Stewart?"

"Yes – I'm here – thank you..."

"Would you like us to freeze your account?"

"No – I'm sorry for the confusion..."

"So everything's okay then?"

"Everything's fine..."

"Is there anything else I can do for you today?"

"Yes – could you give me the name of the bank and the account number I transferred the money to?"

"Yes Sir – you transferred the money to Webster Bank, account number 6712345980..."

"Thank you..."

"Will there be anything else?"

"No – that'll be all for now..."

"Have a good day Mr. Stewart..."

"Same to you..." Sean said as he hung up and then he called Bazil...

"This is Bazil..."

"It's Sean..."

"What's wrong?"

"They got me..."

"Who got you?"

"A couple of grifters..."

"How?"

"I met them at the bar..."

"You had drinks with them?"

"I had drinks with Flick..."

"His name is Flick?"

"That's what he called himself..."

"What happened?"

"His wife..."

"Sean!"

"I know, I know..."

"What happened?"

"I told him I'd give anything to spend the night with a woman as beautiful as she was..."

"Oh my God – Sean – No!"

"He said as long as I let him watch... I could..."

"Come into my web said the spider to the fly..."

"I know Bazil... I know..."

"So you went to their room – did you use any drugs?"

"We drank champagne..."

"They slipped you something..."

"I should've known something was up when security came to my room this morning..."

"Security?"

"He wanted to make sure I was okay – he said I passed out drunk and Mr. Alexander called security to help get me back to my room..."

"Yea – they definitely slipped you something..."

"Isn't that what happened with you and Beautiee?"

"First of all – Beautiee came to my room – second – I made the drink – I'm always in control..."

"You used to be..."

"What the fuck is that supposed to mean?" Bazil snapped...

"Beautiee is the one that's in control..."

"She's in control as much as I allow her to be..."

"If that's what you believe..." Sean laughed...

"You're going off topic..."

"I'm calling you on your bullshit..." Sean laughed...

"Beautiee never took me for anything but my heart..."

"True..."

"How much?"

"$40,000..."

"How did you find out?"

"The bank just called me and told me my transfer was approved..."

"How'd they do it?"

"I requested a new password, I transferred the money, they called to verify the transfer, and I told them there wasn't any fraudulent activity on my account..."

"You mean he did..."

"Yea... he did..."

"Did you remember what I told you?"

"Yes..."

"Thank God – give it to me..."

"Webster Bank - 6712345980..."

"Okay Sean – here's what you need to do..."

"I left the account open..."

"You remembered..."

"You always told me the best way to catch a con is to follow the money..."

"Go on line, put in your username, and request a new password..."

"Why would I do that? They can always request another one after I do..."

"Exactly..."

"And I'll be notified..."

"Exactly..."

"And you'll be able to access their location..."

"So you were listening..."

"Apparently I missed the part where I'm not supposed to go to anyone's room..." Sean sighed...

"I have something to tell you..."

"Okay..."

"Beautiee and I were on our second honeymoon..."

"Okay..."

"Her name was Dontress..."

"Uh huh..."

"She invited us to her room..."

"You went? To her room?"

"We did..."

"What happened?"

"I searched the closets..."

"I bet you did!" Sean exclaimed...

"She asked me if I wanted anything to drink..."

"And you declined... right?"

"Actually... no..."

"No?"

"I went over to the bar, I picked up a bottle, we got in bed with her, and I fucked the shit outta both of them..."

"Beautiee went along with that? How the fuck did you get her to go along with that?"

"I asked her..."

"You asked her? And she said yes?"

"She said yes..."

"You're a lucky son-of-a-bitch – I take back what I said earlier..."

"Thank you..."

"You really think I can get my money back?"

"You'll get some money..."

"Some money?"

"They've done this before – they'll do this again..."

"Ooohhh..."

"And when they do... you'll be waiting for them to cash out... so you can cash in..."

"I feel sorry for them..."

"You do? Why?"

"I hate to see a beautiful woman's life end so tragically – especially one as beautiful as she is..."

"I see..."

"I may have to fuck her first so I'll have something to remember her by..."

"Sean... No..."

"Bazil – you don't understand..."

"Sean... No..."

"Dammit Bazil – she owes me..."

"Sean – what did I tell you?"

"The only sex is consensual sex..." Sean sighed...

"Get some coffee... get some breakfast... and check out – I'll get back to you as soon as we have something..."

"We?"

"Good bye Sean..." Bazil said as he hung up...

"Fine... don't tell me then..." Sean said as he started getting dressed and Bazil picked up the phone and called Sam...

"Sam – I need to see you..."

"I'll be right there..." Sam said and then he hung up... "Yes Bazil?" he asked as he went into Bazil's office...

"Close the door..."

"Okay..." Sam said as he closed the door and sat down...

"This is an account at Webster Bank..." Bazil said as he handed Sam a slip of paper with the account number on it...

"Okay – what do you need?"

"A friend of mine was conned out of $45,000..."

"And they transferred it to this account?"

"Yes..."

"When?"

"Last night..."

"So they're gonna withdraw the money soon..."

"Yes they are..."

"You know who they are?"

"He goes by Flick Alexander..."

"Flick's not his real name..."

"His wife goes by Snow..."

"What hotel is your friend staying at?"

"He didn't tell me – why do you ask?"

"I can access the security footage – if I can see who they are, I can take it from there..." Bazil smiled as he picked up the phone to call Sean on speaker...

"Yes Bazil?"

"What hotel are you staying at?"

"I'm staying at the Wyndham Garden LaGuardia South, Rego Park, NY..."

"What room are you in?"

"I'm in room 723..."

"Okay – thanks – I'll get back to you..." Bazil said as he hung up...

"I'll get right on this..." Sam said as he got up and went back to his office...

CHAPTER THREE

"Okay Flick – since we had to check out before he woke up – can we go home so I can get some sleep?"

"I'm glad you asked me that..." Flick answered as he got in the uber and closed the door...

"You're going to the Hyatt in Yonkers?" the Uber driver asked...

"That's right..." Flick answered...

"Okay..." the driver said as he drove off...

"Yonkers? Baby - why can't we go home?"

"Trust me..."

"Flick – I swear to God – you already know how I am..."

"Yes Sonovia – I know how you are – relax... I gotchu..."

"Whatever..." she sighed. Flick laughed to himself and shook his head. He couldn't wait for Sonovia to see what he had planned...

"We're here..." the driver said. Flick got out and went around to the other side to open the door for his wife... "Come with me..." Flick said as he held out his hand for her to take...

"Alright..." she said as she took his hand and got out...

"C'mon..." Flick said as he pulled Sonovia towards the entrance...

"Okay, okay!" she laughed. She was feeling a little better due to Flick's excitement and Flick smiled when they got to the entrance... "Okay... this is nice..." she said as he held the door for her and she went into the lobby. Flick took her arm, wrapped it around his, and they walked arm-in-arm up to the concierge desk...

"Good evening – welcome to the Hyatt – are you checking in?"

"Yes Maam..." Flick beamed...

"Name please..."

"Sonovia Alexander..." Sonovia looked at him strangely as the woman looked up the information on the computer...

"Found you – let me just print this out... Okay – you're all set..." the clerk said as she handed Sonovia the room keys...

"What time is check out?"

"Check out is 12 p.m...."

"That only gives us a few hours to sleep..." Sonovia sighed...

"We're staying for two nights..." Flick said...

"Oh... Okay!" Sonovia exclaimed...

"What room are we in Babe?"

"713..."

"C'mon – let's go!" Flick exclaimed as he pulled Sonovia towards the elevator...

"Hold on Flick..." Sonovia laughed...

"I can't help it – I'm excited..." Flick said as he pulled her into the elevator. Flick waited for the doors to close and when they did, he startled Sonovia by grabbing her and kissing her hard...

"Damn..." she breathed. The elevator doors opened and Flick took Sonovia by the hand...

"Wait a minute – you're going the wrong way!" Sonovia laughed...

"Sorry about that..." Flick said as he pulled her towards the right direction... "This is the room – gimmie the key!"

"I'll open the door..." Sonovia laughed as she put the key in and unlocked the door... "Oh Flick! This is nice! I love this view!" she exclaimed as she went to look out the window...

"See Baby..." he said as he went up behind Sonovia and kissed her... "I told you..."

"Yea Babe..." she said as she turned around... you told me..." she said as she threw her arms around his neck and kissed him...

"Come with me..." Flick said as he took her by the hand and led her into the bathroom...

"Aww shit – a walk in shower!"

"Uh huh – I'ma walk you in there – I'ma tear your ass up – I'ma walk you over to the bed – and I'ma tear your ass up again..." Flick said as he lifted her arms and pulled her shirt over her head... "Come to Daddy..." he said as he pulled her closer, unhooked her bra, and slid it off her arms...

"Let me help you..." she said as she started to take her thong off and he grabbed her wrists...

"I got this..." Sonovia let go of her thong and Flick took his time sliding his thumbs under the band before he pulled it down. Once it reached her ankles, she stepped out of the thong, moved it to the side, and stood in front of him... "Damn you're sexy..." he breathed as he pulled her into a kiss. Sonovia stood still, anticipating what Flick was going to do next as he took of his shades. He continued looking at her as he took off his shirt and when he pulled it over his head she moved closer and began rubbing his chest. Flick stood still and she took that as her cue to open his pants. She smiled at him mischievously as she pulled his pants and boxers down over his ass, taking her time as she moved his pants and boxers down, making sure she grabbed his ass as they fell down to his ankles. When she saw his dick spring to attention, she began stroking it...

27

"You said something about walking me in here and tearing me up?"

"Let's go..." Flick said as he opened the glass door, stepped inside, guided Sonovia inside, closed the door, pulled her close to him, and turned the shower on full blast...

"Shit! My hair!"

"Baby..." Flick said as he held her under the water with him... "We got $45,000 – I'll get your hair done..." the water was beating down on them as they started kissing profusely. Flick pushed Sonovia back towards the wall, lifted her up, and instinctively she wrapped her arms around his neck and her legs around his back as he guided her onto his dick...

"Oh Flick..." she moaned as he braced himself against the wall, pinning her between the wall and him, as he began thrusting... "Flick... Flick... Flick..." Flick kissed her hard, pushed his tongue in her mouth, and increased his intensity as he fucked her harder...

"Mmmph... Mmmph... Mmmph..."

"Mmm... Mmm... Mmm..." Flick cupped her ass in both hands and held her up against the wall as he guided her to the bench and once he laid her on her back, he put his arms up under her back, pulled her up, and braced his feet against the wall to keep him from sliding as he fucked her deep... "Oh Flick... Fuck... Fuck..."

"Uuugh... Uuugh... Uuugh..."

"I'm cumming... Shit... I'm cumming..."

28

"Uuugh... Uuugh... Uuugh..."

"Aaagh! Aaagh! Aaagh! Aaagh!"

"Uuugh! Uuugh! Uuugh! Uuugh!" Flick lay there for a few moments, kissing her softly, and then he got up, helped her up, and turned her away from him...

"Flick... what..."

"Trust me..." he interrupted. Flick took the KenetMD Luxury Shampoo provided by the Hyatt, poured some in Sonovia's hair, and began massaging her scalp...

"Can I turn around?"

"Turn around..." Sonovia turned around and Flick continued to massage her scalp as he washed her hair... "Now see – you startin' trouble..." he said as Sonovia started playing with his dick...

"I like trouble..." she breathed as his dick got hard in her hand...

"Le'me rinse this out..." he said as he guided her under the water and she closed her eyes. Flick watched the suds flow down her breasts, and he followed them with his hands as they did...

"Ooohhh..." she moaned. Flick took her out from under the water, wiped her eyes, picked up the conditioner, and squirted it in her hair... "Oh my God... your hands..." she moaned as he massaged her scalp. Flick massaged her scalp with the conditioner for a few moments and then he wrapped her hair around her head... "What are you doing?"

"I'm moving your hair out my way..."

"Out your way?"

"The conditioner has to sit in your hair for two minutes..." he said as he handed her a loofah and took one for himself. Flick handed Sonovia the shower gel and she squirted some on the loofah and handed it back to him. He squirted some on the loofah, put the body wash back in place, and they began washing each other. It didn't take long to go from washing each other to being all over each other. Flick pushed Sonovia back under the water as her hair came down, and the conditioner ran down her back as he tilted her head back to kiss her on her neck down to her breasts....

"Oh Flick..." she moaned when he began sucking her breasts. He backed away from her, sat down on the bench, and pulled her pussy to his mouth... "Oh Flick..." she moaned as he pulled her to him by her ass and licked and slurped... "Flick... Oh shit... Flick..." Flick didn't let up and when he pulled her clit in his mouth and sucked it hard, she was done... "FFFLLLIIICCCKKK!" she tried to back away from him but he pulled her pussy right back to his mouth and swirled his tongue around her clit... "HUH... HUH... HUH..." she moaned as he gave her minigasms until she couldn't take anymore... "Flick... stop... I can't..." she panted. Flick stood up and smiled mischievously. Sonovia sat on the bench, pulled his dick to her mouth, and sucked him in down to his balls...

"Oh Shit!" Flick exclaimed as he played in her hair. Sonovia was intent on making him pay by pleasuring him with her mouth as she pulled her mouth off his dick, stroked him, and then took it back in her mouth and down her throat... "Fuck!" Flick moaned as she took her mouth off his dick again and looked up at him...

"Fuck my mouth..." she whispered and then she took his dick in her mouth again. Flick grabbed her on both sides of her head and did as she commanded...

"Shit... Fuck... I'm cummin' Baby... I'm cummin'... UUUGGGHHH!" She continued sucking his dick until he started to buckle... "Okay... Okay..." he panted. Sonovia took her mouth off his dick and looked up at him as Flick pulled her up into his arms and kissed her... "I love you..."

"I love you too..."

"Let's get out and I'll dry your hair..."

"Okay..." she sighed as he led her out the shower and pulled the bench in front of the mirror so she could sit down...

"Sam..."

"Yes Joselyn?"

"It's midnight..."

"I know..."

"Who's so important that you have to call them right now?"

"Bazil..."

"Okay – what's going on?"

"You remember when they embezzled money?"

"Who?"

"Wayne and Mary..."

"They embezzled money?"

"Babe – listen..."

"Okay – I'm listening..."

"Bazil asked me to watch this account and the people that opened it – so I've been monitoring the account and I've been monitoring them too..."

"So you're a spy!" Joselyn exclaimed...

"Something like that..."

"Umm... can you go to jail?"

"Bazil would never put me in a situation where I wind up in jail – but I need to call him – now..."

"You found them?"

"I found them..."

"Oh my God – this is so exciting!"

"You can't say anything..."

"I won't – but call him – I wanna know where they are..."

"Okay – but be quiet..." Sam said as he dialed Bazil's number...

"Bazil – your phone..." Beautiee yawned...

"Sam..." Bazil answered...

"I'm sorry – I know it's late..."

"It's fine – tell me..."

"They're at the Hyatt..."

"Where?"

"Yonkers..."

"So they're still in New York..."

"Yes..."

"Who made the reservation?"

"I'm not sure who made the reservation, but the room is in Sonovia's name..."

"Sonovia? I thought she went by Snow?"

"She does..."

"Any activity on the account?"

"Not yet..."

"What time did they check in?"

"They check in at 10 p.m...."

"When are they checking out?"

"They're booked for two nights..."

"They're going to the casino..."

"I think so too..."

"Thanks Sam..."

"You're welcome..." he said and then he hung up...

"Is everything okay?" Beautiee asked...

"Everything's fine..." Bazil breathed as he put down his phone, turned to Beautiee, and pulled her into a kiss...

"How much did they get?" Joselyn asked...

"They got $45,000..."

"$4,000? Dollars?"

"Joselyn! Keep your voice down!"

"My bad – I'm sorry – I'm just excited!"

"It is exciting..."

"Is he going to have them arrested?"

"They didn't steal it from Bazil – they stole it from Bazil's friend..."

"Well is the friend gonna have them arrested?"

"I don't think so..."

"Wait a minute – they stole $45,000 from him and he doesn't want them arrested? Well what does he – never mind – I'm going to bed – you comin'?"

"Not yet..." Sam answered as he smiled at her mischievously...

"Oh Sam..." Joselyn gushed as he followed her into the bedroom...

CHAPTER FOUR

"Good morning..." Sonovia yawned...

"Good morning..." Flick breathed as he pulled her into a kiss...

"Last night was..."

"Last night was..." Flick said as he got on top of her and spread her legs... "Amazing..." he breathed as he eased himself inside her...

"Flick... I... gottta go..."

"Just le'me get a little..." Flick said as he began fucking her deeper...

"Fuck it..." Sonovia breathed as she pulled Flick down on top of her, grabbed his ass, and threw her pussy back at him...

"Oh shit... that's it Baby – Fuck!" Flick moaned as he quickened his pace...

"Flick... Oh God... Fuck... I'm cumming..."

"Cum for me..."

"Huh... Huh... Huh... Huh..."

"That's it Baby... Give it to me... Uggh! Uggh! Uggh! Uggh!"

"Flick... I... gotta... go..."

"I'm not done with you..." Flick breathed as he pulled out of her and slid down between her legs...

"Flick... I... Ooohhh..." she moaned as he began swirling his tongue around her clit... "Flick... I... Oh shit... Flick... Flick... I'm cummin' again... Huh... Huh... Huh... Oh shit... FFFLLLIIICCCKKK!!" Flick came up from between her legs and to her surprise; he had a huge grin on his face... "Flick... Oh my God... I'm sorry..."

"I'm not..." Flick said as he wiped his face off...

"You're not mad?"

"Mad? For what?"

"Nigga I just peed in your face!" she laughed...

"You just gave me a Golden Shower Baby..." he said as he bent down and kissed her...

"So you really not mad?"

"C'mon – let's go get in the shower – I'm taking you out to breakfast..."

"Okay then..." she sighed as she got up... "Oh shit – look at the bed!" she exclaimed...

"That's what room service is for..." he said as he took her in the bathroom...

"I should 'a came in here when I started to..."

"Didn't I tell you don't worry about it?" he said as he pulled her into a kiss...

"Have you ever had a Golden Shower before?"

"Nope..."

"I never did that before..."

"I keep telling you don't worry about it..."

"I'm glad I didn't do that shit at home..." she said as she got in the shower and turned on the water...

"I might want you to do that shit at home..." he said as he got in the shower with her and closed the door...

"Oh shit – you like that shit!"

"Hell yea I liked that shit!"

"I'on know how I feel about that..."

"Doesn't matter..." he said as he put the body wash on the loofah and started washing himself...

"Da fuck you mean it doesn't matter?" she asked as she did the same...

"Hurry up!" he laughed as he threw water in her face...

"Good morning..." Sean answered...

"Good morning..."

"Did you find them?"

"I did..."

"Where are they?"

"They're in Yonkers..."

"Text me the address..."

"No..."

"No?"

"You need to wait..."

"Wait? For what?"

"Until they get comfortable..."

"Why do I need to wait until they get comfortable?"

"Because once they get comfortable, they'll do it again..."

"What's that got to do with me?"

"You might be able to double your money..."

"Okay... I'll wait a couple of days..."

"I'll keep you posted..."

"Thank you Bazil..."

"Flick – look at the bed!" Sonovia exclaimed as they were getting dressed. Flick went over to the bed and snatched off the spread, the blanket, and the sheets... "What are you doing?"

"I'ma take care of it..." he answered as he tossed the pillows onto the chaise lounge and turned over the mattress...

"So... what are you gonna tell them?"

"Don't worry about it – get dressed so I can feed you..."

"Okay..." she sighed as she got dressed. Flick watched her intently... "What's wrong – you

38

want me to change?" Flick didn't answer her – he just got up off the bed, walked over to her, and kissed her...

"I love you too..."

"Good – let's go – the Uber will be downstairs in 5 minutes..." he said as he took her hand and led her out into the corridor... "Excuse me – miss?"

"Yes sir?"

"My wife and I had a little too much fun last night – we spilled champagne all over the sheets – I had to take them off the bed..."

"What room are you in?"

"713..."

"I'll take care of it..."

"Thank you – I appreciate that..." he said as he slipped a $20 bill in her apron...

"Thank you..."

"You're welcome..." he said as he pulled Sonovia towards the elevator...

"Okay – that was good   I feel better now..." she breathed...

"I told you I'd take care of it..." he said as the elevator doors opened and they walked through the lobby and out the entrance. Flick opened the door for Sonovia, waited for her to get in, and closed the door. The Uber had plexiglass high as the taxis used to be and just as thick so they didn't have to worry about putting a mask on...

CHAPTER FIVE

"Okay "I-Hop?""

"Yes..." Flick answered...

"Okay..." the driver said as he drove off...

"Oh my God – I haven't been to I-Hop in years!"

"I know..." Flick smiled...

"I'ma bust those Harvest Grain Nut Pancakes down!"

"I'ma bust that steak omelet down!" he laughed...

"This is really nice – thank you Babe..."

"You're welcome..." he said as he took her hand and kissed it...

"We're here..." the driver said...

"Thank you..." Flick said as he got out. Flick went around to the other side, opened the door for Sonovia, she got out, and he took her by the hand and walked her to the front door...

"Flick – we don't have any masks..."

"Yes we do..." he said as he took two masks out his pocket. After they put the masks on, they went inside... "Damn – how long is the wait?"

"Table for two?" the hostess asked...

"Yes Maam..." Flick answered...

"Name?"

"Alexander..."

"It'll be about 30 minutes..."

"Damn – well I guess that's not too bad..." she sighed as she went to sit beside another woman...

"Good morning..." the woman said...

"Good morning..."

"I'm Mary..." she said as she held out her hand...

"I'm Sonovia – sorry I can't shake your hand..." she said as she put out her arm so they could bump arms...

"I'll be glad when this is over so we can be normal again..."

"I don't think we'll ever be normal again..." Sonovia laughed...

"I think you're right..."

"Holloway – party of two..." the hostess called...

"That's us – it was nice meeting you..."

"Nice meeting you too..."

"Hey Babe – who was that?" Flick asked as he sat down next to her...

"That was Mary – she's nice..."

"Oh yea?"

"Yea – why?"

"Her husband was checking you out the whole time you were talkin'..."

"I know you lyin'!"

"Excuse me – Sonovia?" Mary interrupted...

"Yes?"

"I asked my husband if I could invite you to sit with us... if that's alright..."

"Uh... I dunno..."

"Do it Babe..." Flick urged...

"You sure?"

"I'm sure..." he answered as he stood up...

"Okay..." Sonovia said as she got up and they went to sit at the table...

"You must be Sonovia..." he said as he tried to take her hand...

"Uh uh – covid..."

"I'm sorry – I forgot..." he laughed...

"I'm Flick..." Flick said as he sat down next to her husband...

"I'm Aiden – and this is my wife Mary..."

"Nice to meet you Mary..."

"Sonovia... that's a beautiful name..." Mary said...

"Thank you – my friends call me Snow..."

"Snow... I like that..."

"So do I..." Aiden said. Flick was annoyed and was ready to leave the table but Sonovia was engaged in conversation with Mary so he decided to stay...

"We love I-Hop..."

"So do we – right Flick?"

"Yea Babe..." he answered. Flick smiled to himself because he had Aiden pinned in the corner...

"Welcome to I-Hop – may I take your order?" the waitress asked...

"Coffee for the table..." Aiden answered...

"Okay – I'll be right back..." she said as she went to get the coffee..."

"Are you going to the casino later?" Aiden asked as he turned to Flick...

"Yea..."

"Are you staying at the Hyatt?" Mary asked...

"Yes..." Sonovia answered...

"Oh that's nice – maybe we can get together later for dinner..."

"We'll see..." Flick said as the waitress came back with the coffee...

"Okay – are we ready to order?"

"Ladies first..." Flick said...

"I'll have a regular breakfast – but I want the Harvest Grain Pancakes..." Sonovia said...

"Okay – scrambled with bacon or sausage/'

"Bacon..."

"I'll have the same..." Mary said...

"I'll have the steak omelet..." Flick said...

"Regular pancakes or wheat pancakes?"

"Regular..."

"I'll have the same thing – wheat pancakes..." Aiden said...

"Okay – I'll be back..." she said as she left to place the order...

"I don't gamble..." Mary said as she took off her mask and made herself a cup of coffee...

"Not even the slot machines?" Sonovia asked as she went to pick up the pot...

"Le'me get that for you..." Flick said as he poured coffee for her, Aiden, and himself...

"Never tried it..."

"I love it..."

"You do?"

"Sit by me tonight – I usually pick winners..."

"Okay – I'll do that..." Mary said. Flick noticed how Aiden was looking at Sonovia's breasts and under any other circumstances he'd go off - but this time he smiled to himself...

"Here's your breakfast..." the waitress said as she began putting the food on the table...

"Thank you, thank you, thank you..." they all said...

"If you need anything else, just let me know..." the waitress said as she left to take another order...

"Flick – what's your game?" Aiden asked...

"Black jack..."

"No Kidding?"

"I don't bother with the slot machines..." Flick answered as they continued eating...

"You do alright at the tables?"

"I do alright..." Flick answered...

"I guess you do alright on the slot machines..." Mary laughed...

"I do alright..."

"So you never lose?"

"Sometimes I win, sometimes I break even..." They continued eating without speaking...

"How's everything going?" the waitress asked...

"Good... good..."

"Ready for the check?"

"I'll take it..." Aiden said...

"Aww – thank you!" Sonovia exclaimed...

"My pleasure..." Aiden said. The waitress went to get the check and when she handed the bill to Aiden, he pulled out a Chase Sapphire card and stuck it in the bill holder. Flick could barely contain his excitement...

"Here you are..." the waitress said as she handed Aiden his card...

"You guys need a ride back to the hotel?" Aiden asked...

"Thanks – but we're going shopping..." Flick answered...

"Okay – we'll see you later tonight..." Aiden said...

"Here..." Mary said as she handed a card to Sonovia with the room number on it... "Give us a call later..."

"Okay..." Sonovia said as they left...

"Sonovia – the Uber's here..." Flick said...

"I thought you said we were going shopping?"

"I just said that cause I didn't wanna get in the car with him..."

"So we're not going shopping?"

"Baby – I'll take you shopping when we get back to Cross County..." he said as the Uber pulled up...

CHAPTER SIX

"Cross County?" the Uber driver asked...

"Macy's" Flick answered as they both got in and closed the door...

"Ooohhh... I like Macys..." Sonovia beamed as the driver drove off. When they got to Macy's, she didn't wait for Flick to open the door...

"You excited Babe?"

"Hell yea I'm excited – let's go!" she exclaimed as she took his hand and pulled him inside. As soon as they put their masks on, the associate was right on them...

"Would you like to try some perfume?" she asked...

"Sure..." Sonovia answered as she held out her wrists...

"This is Obsession..." she said as she sprayed her left wrist... "And this one is Daisy..." she said as she sprayed her right wrist..."

"You already know I like Daisy..." Sonovia laughed as she looked at Flick...

"You want it?"

"Yea..."

"Get it..."

"Okay – would you like the small bottle or the large bottle?" the associate asked...

"I'll take the small one – I don't wanna have to worry about the large one breaking in my bag..."

"Okay – I'll ring that right up for you..." she said as she rung up the sale... "Here you go – thank you for shopping at Macy's..." she said as she handed Sonovia the bag...

"Thank you Baby..." Sonovia said as she gave Flick a kiss...

"You're welcome – excuse me Miss – where's your lingerie department?"

"That's on the 3rd floor..."

"Thanks – c'mon..." Flick said as he took Sonovia's hand and took her towards the escalator...

"Flick – wait..." she said as she stopped in the jewelry section. Flick didn't say anything – he just bust out laughing... "I can't have any jewelry?"

"You can have whatever you want..."

"How can I help you?" the associate asked as she hurried over to Sonovia...

"Well... since my husband said I can have anything I want... I want the Northern Lights Bracelet..."

"I love that bracelet – it's made with Swarovski Crystals..."

"I know..."

"Let me take it out the case for you..." the associate said as she took the bracelet out and put it on Sonovia's wrist...

"Oh wow – look Flick..." she sighed...

"It's beautiful..." the associate agreed...

"I'll take it..."

"Okay – I'll wrap it up for you..." the associate said. Sonovia put her wrist on the counter and sighed... "I know how you feel – I wouldn't want to take it off either..." she said as she took it off and boxed it up... "Here you go..." the associate said as she handed the bag to Sonovia...

"Thank you Baby..." Sonovia said as she went to Flick and gave him a kiss...

"You're welcome – c'mon..." Flick said as he pulled Sonovia to the escalator...

"I'm coming..." she laughed...

"Not yet – but you will be..." Flick said as he put her on the escalator in front of him so he could stand behind her on the escalator and hold her around her waist. As soon as he got off the escalator he saw what he liked... "Get that..." he said as he pointed to the Red Unwrap Me Satin Bow Teddy..."

"I thought you said I could get whatever I want?"

"You can..."

"Oh so you wanna unwrap me?"

"Oh yea..."

"Okay – le'me see if they have my size..." she said as she looked through them...

"Need any help?" the associate asked...

"No thanks – I got it..." Sonovia said...

"Oh – Sonovia – get this!" Flick exclaimed when he saw the Red Scalloped Trim Floral Lace Garter Lingerie set...

"Oh my – that's very popular – I'll bring an extra-large..." the associate said as she went to get it...

"She didn't even ask me what size I wear – I'm offended..." Sonovia laughed...

"How's this?" the associate asked when she came back with the set...

"Oh that'll fit me – look Flick..." she said as she put the cup over her breast...

"We'll take that..." Flick said with a smile...

"I'll right it right up..." the associate said as she went over to the register...

"Can I get an outfit?"

"Sure..."

"Okay – cause I can't wear what you bought me outside..." she laughed...

50

"Here ya go – enjoy..." the associate said as she handed Sonovia the bag...

"Thank you Babe – c'mon..." she said as she pulled Flick towards the escalator...

"You know where you goin'?"

"Yea – downstairs..." she answered as she got on the escalator and Flick got on behind her. When they got downstairs Sonovia saw what she wanted right away... "I want these!" she exclaimed as she picked up a pair of Wanna Betta Butt Jeans...

"Okay – what shirt you want?"

"I want this Seamless Fitted Cut Out Top..."

"I like that..."

"Me too..."

"Go try it on..."

"Okay..." Sonovia said as she handed Flick the bags. Flick sat in the chair and waited for her to come out and when she did he was all smiles...

"Babe – turn around..." Sonovia turned around for him...

"You like?"

"I like..."

"So do I..." another man laughed as he walked by...

"That's mine!" Flick exclaimed...

"My bad – no disrespect..." the man said as Sonovia walked back into the dressing room...

"How's everything going?" the associate said as she came over...

"I'm just waiting for my wife..." Flick answered as Sonovia came over...

"Everything okay Miss?" she asked...

"Everything's fine – oh wait – do you have those boots in my size?"

"What size are you?"

"6 Medium..."

"Let me check..." the associate said as she went to check for the boots...

"You're in luck..." she said as she brought the boots out...

"Thank you!" Sonovia exclaimed...

"You're welcome – would you like me to ring that up for you?"

"Yes – thank you..."

"Okay – I'll be right back..." she said as she went to ring everything up... "Here you go – thank you for shopping at Macy's..."

"Thank you Baby..."

"You're welcome – c'mon – let's go back to the hotel so you can put on that nightie and I can unwrap you..." he said as he pulled Sonovia into a kiss...

When they got back to the hotel, Sonovia looked at the bed and smiled... "Look Flick..."

"What?"

"The bed..."

"Oh nice! I thought they were just gonna change the sheets!"

"Me too..."

"Come sit down – I wanna talk to you..."

"Okay..."

"Aiden was watching you..."

"Flick – I don't want him!" she laughed...

"I know that – but he wants you..."

"What are you saying?"

"I want you to put on that garter set...and I wanna invite him here..."

"Hell no! I'm not wearing that shit for another man – why the fuck would you ask me to do that?!"

"I don't want you to wear it for him – I just want him to see you in it..."

"Da Fuck?"

"I want you to come out the bathroom – by accident – on purpose..."

"So... you want me to put that lingerie on... you want me to act like I don't know he's here... and you want me to come out the bathroom?"

"Just for a second..."

"Oh shit! We gonna get him?"

"We're gonna get him..."

"What about his wife?"

"She'll be here..."

"How the fuck..."

"Sonovia... listen..." Flick interrupted...

"Okay – I'm listening..."

"We're gonna meet them in the casino – you hang out with Mary for a little bit – then you come to the tables – then we invite them back to our room..."

"How am I going to come out in lingerie by accident?"

"I'll tell them to come at 10:30 – you come out and apologize – you thought it was 10:00 – you didn't realize the time – while you're doing that – I'll make the champagne..."

"What about his wife?"

"She'll be watching her husband..."

"What if they don't have any money?"

"He paid the check at I-Hop with a Sapphire..."

"What's a Sapphire?"

"That's a card issued by Chase Bank..."

"A credit card?"

"It comes with a $50,000 credit limit – you can't qualify for that unless you have money..."

"Shit – that's dangerous..."

"Especially in your hands..."

"Shut up Flick!" she said and then they both laughed...

"You have that card she gave you?" he asked...

"Yea..."

"Go use the phone – call the room – tell Mary we'll meet them downstairs at 7..."

"Okay..." Sonovia said as she got up and went to call them...

"Hello?"

"Mary – it's Snow..."

"Hi Snow! Did you enjoy shopping?"

"I did..."

"You must be tired – are we still going to the casino?"

"Yes – we'll meet you in the lobby at 7..."

"Okay – we'll see you then..."

"We good?" Flick asked...

"We're good..."

"Now..." he said as he got up, went over to Sonovia, pulled her up into his arms, and kissed her... "I want you to go in the bathroom..." he breathed as he kissed her... "Put on your ribbon..." he breathed as he kissed her again... "Come get in this bed..." he breathed as he kissed her again... "And let me unwrap you..."

CHAPTER SEVEN

"You sure about this?" Sonovia asked as she started getting dressed...

"Turn around..." Flick commanded... "Damn you look good..."

"I don't want him to see me in this Flick..."

"It'll just be a second..."

"I should be wearing this for my husband..." she sighed...

"You are Baby..." Flick said as he got up and went over to her...

"He better have some fuckin' money!" she laughed as she put on the outfit Flick bought earlier...

"Look at dat ass!" he exclaimed as he slapped her on her ass...

"Ouch!"

"I'm sorry Baby..." he breathed as he pulled her into a kiss..."

"Le'me hurry up and put these boots on so we can do this..." she said as she sat down. When she got up and started walking, her ass giggled and Flick was mesmerized... "Are you coming?"

"Not yet – but I will be..." he answered as he got up and they went downstairs...

"Snow! You look great!" Mary exclaimed...

"Thank you..."

"You look lovely..." Aiden said...

"She does – doesn't she?" Flick asked as he wrapped his arm around Sonovia and walked her up ahead of them, making sure her ass was in Aiden's eyesight. When they got outside, the car was waiting and Flick opened the door...

"Nice car..." Sonovia said as she got in...

"Thank you..." Aiden said. Flick opened the door for Mary and she got in...

"Thank you Flick..."

"You're welcome..." Flick said as he closed the door. Aiden watched Flick as he went around to the other side and got in before he got in himself... "This is nice..." he said as Aiden drove off...

"Thank you – I love this car..."

"I'm a Mercedes man too..."

"You are? Which model?"

"CLA-Class..."

"We looked at that one too – but my wife fell in love with this one..."

"I sure did..." Mary acknowledged...

"Doesn't matter to me – as long as it's a Mercedes..." Sonovia laughed...

"We're here..." Aiden said as they pulled up in front of Empire...

"I can't wait to go inside!" Mary exclaimed...

"Since when?" Aiden asked... "You've never been excited about gambling..."

"I've never met anyone that was interested in showing me how to play..." she said as she opened the door to get out and the valet opened the door for her... "Thank you..." she said as she got out. Flick got out and went to open the door for Sonovia as Aiden handed his keys to the valet...

"Ready?" Aiden asked as he put his mask on...

"Ready!" they answered in unison as they put their masks on and headed inside...

"C'mon..." Sonovia said as she hooked her arm in Mary's arm...

"See you later Babe..." Flick said...

"You didn't tell your wife where we'll be..." Aiden said...

"She'll find me..." Flick said as he walked over to the table and Aiden followed...

"Where do I start?" Mary asked...

"I'll give you a tour..."

"Oh look – penny machines!" she exclaimed...

"Stay away from those..."

"Why?"

"See that?' Sonovia asked as she pointed to a woman jumping up and down...

"I see! She won!"

"She won 5,000 pennies..."

"Oh wow!"

"That's $50.00..."

"That's nice!"

"Why put a dollar in a penny machine to win $50 when you can put a dollar in a $1 machine and win $500 or $5,000?"

"Oh... I see..."

"These are the quarter machines..."

"Okay..."

"Here's the thing – you won't win a whole lot if you play a quarter at a time, so you need to play at least a dollar at a time..."

"Like the $1 machine?"

"Here's where they get you – you put $10 - $20 in the quarter machine – you play for a while – you win some – then you start losing – you try to win your money back – next thing you know – you lost $10 - $20.00..."

"That's not too bad..."

"That's not too bad for you if you get up and cut your losses – but if you put another $10 - $20 in the machine..."

"Ooohhh..."

"Now you might be the lucky one..."

"How do I know if I'm the lucky one?"

"You don't sit down right away – you walk around for a little while – you watch – and you'll see somebody get up from a machine because they've been playing for a while and they haven't hit..."

"Ooohhh..."

"Here's another thing – always look for a machine that has a progressive jackpot..."

"Why's that?"

"Because every time somebody puts money in the machine, the jackpot goes up until somebody hit it..."

"Ooohhh..."

"Let's get those two machines – you get the left seat – I'll get the right..." Sonovia said as they went over to the seats and they sat down...

"How do you know these are winners?" Mary yelled...

"The jackpot is up to $150,000..."

"Okay! Let's Play!" she exclaimed as she took out a $100 bill...

"Hole up – don't put that much in there!"

"Okay – how much should I put in the machine?"

"Start with $20.00 – see how you do..."

"Okay!" Mary exclaimed as she started to play...

"Table is closed..." the dealer said as he spun the wheel... "34 Black!"

"Shit!" Aiden exclaimed as he threw his hands up in disgust. Flick smiled as he pulled his chips towards him... "How the fuck do you do that?"

"I bet the numbers that haven't come up yet..."

"You can keep track of the numbers?"

"Yea..."

"Place your bets..." the dealer said...

"I'm done..." Flick said as he picked up his chips...

"I'm in – 50 Red..." Aiden said...

"Table is closed..." the dealer said as he spun the wheel... "64 Red!"

"Shit!" Aiden cursed again as he threw up his hands in disgust...

"Just one more..." Mary pleaded...

"Mary – stop!"

"Okay!" Mary huffed as she cashed out...

"I'ma tell you a story..."

"Okay..."

"Last year – this woman won $3,000.00 playing the dollar machine..."

"Okay..."

"She played it all back..."

"Ooohhh..."

"C'mon..." Sonovia said as she wrapped her arm around Mary's arm and walked her over to the tables...

"Hey Babe..." Flick said as he pulled his wife into a hug...

"Hey..."

"You good?"

"I won $5,000..."

"That's what I'm talkin' about!" Flick exclaimed...

"How'd you do Aiden?" Mary asked...

"You don't wanna know..." he sighed...

"That much?"

"Yea..."

"I won $3,000!"

"That's great Honey..." Aiden said as he pulled her into a hug. Flick knew Aiden was faking it...

"C'mon – let's go cash out..." Flick said as he put the chips in his pocket and they all went to the cashier...

"Next..."

"Go ahead Mary..." Sonovia said...

"I won!" Mary exclaimed...

"Congratulations – ticket and I.D. please..."

"Here ya go..."

"How would you like it?"

"Cash..."

"How would you like it?"

"Sonovia – what do I say?"

"100's..."

"Okay..." the cashier said as she counted out the money... "There you go Maam..."

"Thank you!" Mary exclaimed as she held up the money...

"Uh uh!" Sonovia snapped... "Put that money away – you don't know who's watching you!"

"Sorry – I'm not used to this..." Mary said as she put the money in her purse...

"Next!" Sonovia went up to the cashier and put her ticket and I.D. on the counter... "Congratulations..."

"Thank you..."

"How would you like it?"

"$1,000.00 cash – the rest in a check..."

"You can do that?" Mary asked...

"Yes..." Sonovia answered as the cashier counted out the cash and she put it in her front pocket...

"It'll be just a few minutes for the check..." the cashier said...

"That's fine..." Sonovia said...

"Here ya go..." the cashier said as she placed the check down on the counter...

"Thank you..." Sonovia said as she took the check and put it in her other side pocket...

"Next!"

"Here Babe..." Flick said as he gave her the chips...

"Here you go..." Sonovia said as she put her I.D. on the counter again...

"Congratulations again..."

"Thank you..."

"You have $50,000.00"

"Oh my God!" Mary exclaimed...

"Don't do that!" Sonovia exclaimed...

"Sorry..."

"Everybody don't need to know our business..."

'I'm sorry – I'm just happy for you..."

"I know – but people case casinos, watch and listen..."

"How do you know all this?"

"True Crime..."

"The television show?"

'Yea..."

"Ms. Alexander – I'm just waiting on the manager to come and approve your check..." the cashier interrupted...

"Thank you – I can wait..."

"I didn't know you won that much..." Aiden said...

"I thought you knew..." Flick lied...

"I was too busy counting my losses..." Aiden sighed...

"Ms. Alexander – I need you to come with me..." an officer said as he approached...

"Is there a problem?"

"Not at all – I just need to escort you inside so you can sign for your check..."

"I didn't have to sign for the other check..."

"We require signatures for checks over $10,000..."

"Can my husband come with me?"

"I'm sorry – we only escort the person signing the check – it'll just be a moment..." he said as he guided her towards the door and they went inside...

"Ms. Alexander – is there a reason your husband didn't turn this in?" the manager asked...

"No reason..."

"Your husband was pretty lucky tonight..."

"He was..."

"Is your husband always this lucky?"

"You think my husband cheated you out of money?"

"No..." the manager answered as he signed the check... "Just sign here and you're all set..." the manager said as he handed her a paper to sigh. Sonovia signed the paper and the manager handed her the check...

"Thank you..." she said as she put the check in her pocket...

"Okay – let's get you back to your husband..." the officer said as he escorted her back out by the cashier...

"You good?" Flick asked...

"I'm good..." Sonovia answered...

"Enjoy your evening..." the officer said as he left them...

"Anybody hungry?" Aiden asked...

"I'm hungry..." Mary said...

"I guess we could go get something to eat..." Flick answered...

"Let's go to The Pub..." Aiden said...

"The Pub?" Flick repeated...

"Good food, good drinks, and it's near the valet entrance...

"Okay..." Flick said as he took Sonovia's hand and they followed Aiden and Mary to the Pub...

"Welcome to the Pub – can I start you out with something to drink?" the server asked...

"I'll have a Merlot..." Mary answered...

"I'll have a Pinot Grigio..." Sonovia answered...

"I'll have a Heineken..." Flick answered...

"Will that be a glass or a bottle?"

"Bottle..."

"I'll have the same..." Aiden answered...

"Okay – I'll be right back..." she said as she left...

"I see what I want already..." Sonovia said...

"What Babe?" Flick asked...

"Bacon cheddar burger..."

"I'ma get the philly steak sandwich..." Flick said...

"I'm getting the ribeye steak..." Aiden said...

"I'm getting the blackened salmon..." Mary said as the server came back with the drinks...

"Are you ready to order?" the server asked...

"Ribeye steak, blackened salmon, philly steak sandwich, and a bacon cheddar burger..." Aiden answered...

"Okay – how would you like that cooked?"

"Medium well..."

"Aiden – you shouldn't eat steak undercooked..." Mary said...

"I said Medium well – not medium rare..." Aiden laughed...

"How 'bout the burger?" the server asked...

"Well done..." Sonovia answered...

"Okay – I'll be back..." she said as she went to place the order...

"When are you leaving?" Aiden asked...

"Tomorrow..." Flick answered...

"Oh shoot – I wish you could stay one more day – I'd like to spend more time with Snow..." Mary sighed...

"Why don't you come up to our room later tonight?" Flick asked...

"What time?" Aiden asked...

"About 10:30?"

"That's past my wife's bedtime..."

"I'll be fine as long as I get a nap in..." Mary said...

"Okay – we'll be there..." Aiden said as the server came back with the food...

"That was fast..." Sonovia said...

"It sure was..." Mary said as she began eating... "Oh my God – this salmon is delicious!"

"So is this burger..." Sonovia laughed. Flick and Aiden were tearing their food down as they all continued to eat...

"How's everything?" the server asked as she came over...

"Mmm hmmm..." they answered as they continued eating...

"Damn that was good!" Aiden exclaimed...

"I guess you were hungry!" Flick laughed...

"I love a good steak..." Aiden said as he rubbed his stomach...

"Would you like any dessert?" the server asked as she came back over to the table...

"I don't have any room..."Flick answered...

"Me either..." Aiden answered...

"Me either..." Sonovia answered...

"And you miss?" the server asked Mary...

"No thank you..."

"Okay – I'll be right back with your check..." she said as she walked away...

"I'm going to sleep really good tonight..." Mary sighed...

"Here's your check..." the server said as she placed it on the table...

"Here..." Flick said as he put his credit card in the bill holder...

"I'll be right back..." the server said as she walked away...

"Thanks Flick..." Aiden said...

"You're welcome..." Flick said as the server came back...

"Here you go..." she said as she gave Flick his card...

"Thank you..." Flick said as he got up and held out his hand to help Sonovia up...

"Are you ready Mary?" Aiden asked as he got up and extended his hand to help Mary up...

"I'm ready..."

"Let's go..." Aiden said as they put their masks on and followed him out to the valet...

"Thanks for dinner – we'll see you at 10:30" Aiden said as he took Mary by the hand and started to walk off...

"Aiden – wait..." Mary said...

"What's wrong?"

"We don't know their room number..." Mary laughed...

"713..." Sonovia said...

"Got it – we'll see you later..." Aiden said as he pulled Mary by the hand...

"I guess he's in a hurry..." Sonovia laughed...

"He's goin' to get some pussy..." Flick laughed as they got in the elevator and went upstairs to their room...

CHAPTER EIGHT

"Oh shit – what time is it?" Sonovia exclaimed as she jumped up...

"It's 10 o'clock..." Flick yawned as he got up...

"Flick... I've been thinking..."

"Uh oh..."

"I don't wanna do this..."

"I knew it..."

"Something doesn't feel right..."

"You don't wanna do this 'cause you like Mary..."

"Yea... I do..."

"She's nice – but we didn't come here to make friends..."

"I'on know Flick – can't I just wear what I'm wearing?"

"Wait – what are you talking about?"

"I don't wanna come out in the garter outfit..."

"Oh shit – I thought you wanted to call off the whole thing!" Flick laughed...

"I don't wanna call it off... but..."

"See – I knew it – you like Mary!"

"I do!"

"What if you never met her?"

"But I did meet her...

"You want me to call it off?"

"I don't know..."

"Look – it's 10 after – whatchu want me to do?"

"Do it – but I'm keeping my clothes on..." she answered as she went to the bathroom...

"I might as well throw some water on my face..." he said as he followed her into the bathroom...

"They're not answering the phone..." Mary said...

"Maybe they're still asleep..." Aiden said...

"I sure hope not – I really wanna spend some time with them before they check out tomorrow..."

"C'mon – we'll go check on them..." Aiden said as they left their room and headed to the elevator...

"Who is it?" Sonovia asked as they hurried out the bathroom and fixed their clothes...

"It's me Snow..." Mary answered...

"I'll be right there..." Sonovia said as she went to open the door and Flick went to open the bottle of champagne...

"Hi Snow..." Mary sighed...

"Hi Mary, Hi Aiden – come in..." she said as she opened the door...

"Hey Flick..." Aiden said as he came in...

"Hey Aiden – I'll be right with y'all..." he said as he turned to look at Aiden and then went back to pouring the champagne...

"Look at this view!" Mary exclaimed as she went over to the window...

"It certainly is beautiful..." Aiden said as he walked over to look out the window. Flick took two melatonin tablets out his pocket, dropped them in the first two glasses, and stood up from the chair...

"Here ya go..." Flick said as he handed the first two glasses to Aiden and Mary...

"Oh – I don't drink champagne..." Mary said...

"Mary – one glass won't hurt..." Aiden laughed...

"It may not hurt – but you may have to carry me..." Mary laughed...

"Then I'll carry you..." Aiden said as he looked at her seductively. Flick picked up the other glasses of champagne, handed one to Sonovia, and then he raised his glass...

"To friends..."

"To friends..." they all said and then they all took a sip...

"That's enough for me..." Mary laughed...

"Mary – it's just one glass!" Aiden laughed...

"Oh what the hell – I guess I can sleep it off..." she laughed as she gulped it down...

"That's better..." Aiden said and then he gulped his down... "What's a matter Flick – you not thirsty?"

"Oh yea..." Flick answered as he finished his glass and set it down on the table. Sonovia watched them both as she continued to sip on her glass...

"Oh my goodness..." Mary giggled...

"What's wrong Mary?" Aiden laughed...

"I think it's gone to my head already..."

"C'mon..." Aiden said as he led Mary over to the couch, sat her down, and sat down beside her. Flick went to sit down beside Aiden and Sonovia sat next to Mary... "So... you live in the area?" Aiden yawned...

"No – we live in Queens..." Flick answered...

"They have... a... casino out there?" Flick smiled as he could tell the melatonin was working......

"Yea – Resorts World – Ozone Park..."

"You okay Mary?" Sonovia asked...

"Mmm hmmm..." she mumbled as she closed her eyes...

"I've never been to that casino... I..." Aiden stopped mid-sentence as he drifted off...

"Are they sleep?" Sonovia whispered...

"Yea..." Flick whispered...

"Let's go look out the window..." Sonovia whispered...

"Okay..." Flick whispered as he got up...

"I just wanna make sure they really sleep..." Sonovia whispered...

"We'll give it another 5 minutes..." Flick whispered as he pulled Sonovia into a hug and kissed her. After standing there for a little over 5 minutes Flick spoke... "Go turn on the laptop...

"Okay..." she whispered as she went over to the table, sat down, and turned on the laptop...

"Hey Aiden..." Flick whispered as he sat down beside him, eased his cell phone out his pocket, and eased his wallet out his back pocket. When Aiden didn't move, Flick checked to see if he still had a pulse... "Okay – go to chase.com..." he whispered. Sonovia typed it in the browser... "Put in Holloway Properties..."

"Okay..."

"Password $Holloway1 – capital H..."

"He put his password on the back of his card?"

"Yup..." Flick answered as Sonovia logged in...

"Oh shit – Flick – this some bullshit!" she exclaimed in a whisper. Flick went over to the computer, looked on the screen, and bust out laughing... "Sshhh!"

"Log off..."

"Can't we just..."

"Please – it's only $5,000.oo – it's not even worth it..."

"What about his card?"

"Sonovia – look at the balance..."

"Oh shit!"

"Exactly..."

"How you have a fifty thousand dollar credit limit and you charged up to $45,000?"

"We couldn't even get a cash advance off that shit..."

"Damn!" Sonovia exclaimed as she logged off...

"You think you can get Mary back to her room by yourself?"

"Why I gotta do it by myself?"

"Cause I'ma have him..."

"Wait a minute – I have an idea..." she said as she called the front desk...

"Front desk – may I help you?"

"Do you have any wheel chairs?"

"Yes Maam – is everything alright?"

"Yea – my friends feeling a little light headed and she needs help getting back to her room..."

"Do you need an ambulance?"

"Oh no – she just had a little too much champagne..." Sonovia laughed...

"Okay – we'll send someone right up..."

"Thank you..."

"They're sending someone up?" Flick asked...

"Yea..."

"Oh shit – I think that's them..." Flick said as he heard a knock on the door...

"Who is it?"

"You asked for a wheelchair?"

"Be right there..." Flick said as he got up to open the door...

"Here you go – you can bring it back down to the lobby when you're finished with it..." the bellman said as Flick took the wheelchair... "Have a good night..." he said as he left...

"Okay – you take her first..."

"Na... you take him first..."

"Okay..." Flick said as he opened the wheel chair... "C'mon Aiden..." Flick said as he lifted Aiden up off the couch and into the wheelchair...

"Wwwhhhaattsss... goin'... on?" Aiden slurred...

"I'm just helping you back to your room..." Flick answered as he put Aiden's cell phone and wallet in his pocket... "I'll be right back..." Flick said as he pushed Aiden out the room and down the hall to the elevator. Sonovia waited

76

anxiously as she kept watching the door... "I'm back..." Flick said as he came in...

"Everything okay?"

"He's in bed – sleeping like a baby..."

"Good – now for Mary..." she said as she got up...

"I got her..." Flick said as he picked Mary up in his arms and put her in the wheelchair...

"Mary? Sonovia called...

"Wwwwhhhaat... wwwhhhaaattt...time... is... it?" she slurred...

"It's time for you to go to bed..." Sonovia laughed...

"Where... where..."

"Your husband is waiting for you..." Sonovia said as she began pushing her out the room...

"Is she alright?" a man asked when they saw Sonovia and Mary...

"She's fine..."

"She doesn't look fine..."

"Harold – mind your business!" the woman exclaimed as Sonovia got on the elevator and they went downstairs. When they got off the elevator Sonovia hurried Mary to her room and used the room key in Mary's pocket to open the door...

"Okay Mary – it's time for you to go to bed..." she said as she helped Mary up out the wheel chair and helped her over to the bed. Mary crawled up beside her husband and went right to sleep... "Thank God..." Sonovia breathed as she folded the wheelchair up, rolled it out the room, and closed the door behind her... "Can you take this for me?" she asked when she saw the bellman...

"Sure..." he answered as he came and took the wheelchair from her...

"Thank you..."

"You're welcome..." Sonovia went to the elevator, got in, and went back upstairs to their room...

"All good?" Flick asked...

"All good..." she breathed as she started getting undressed. Flick watched her intently. After she stripped down to the garter outfit she strutted in front of him and stood in front of the window...

"Bring that sexy ass over here..." he commanded...

"Come get this sexy ass..." she commanded. Flick stood up, went over to the window, and grabbed her by her waist... "Take off your clothes..." she commanded. Flick stepped back from her, stripped down, and waited. Sonovia turned to face the window, put her arms up, braced herself on the window, and spread her legs, giving Flick a full view and complete access. Flick smiled mischievously as he went behind her, eased himself inside her, and fucked her from behind as they both continued to look out the window...

CHAPTER NINE

"Good morning..." Aiden yawned...

"What the hell happened last night?" Mary yawned...

"I have no idea..."

"I need coffee..." Mary said as she got up and put on her robe...

"Mary – where are you going?"

"I'm going to the cafeteria to get some coffee..."

"Wait a sec..." Aiden said as he got up... "I'll come with ya..."

"C'mon..." she said as she opened the door and they went out into the hall... "Excuse me..." Mary said...

"Yes?" Harold answered...

"I see you have coffee – do they still have some left?"

"Oh yea – they just made it..."

"Thank you..."

"I'm glad to see you're feeling better..."

"I beg your pardon?" Aiden asked...

"Your wife was being pushed in a wheelchair last night to her room – she didn't look well..." Harold answered...

"Oh my goodness – Aiden – I told you I shouldn't have had any champagne..." Mary laughed...

"I guess not..." Aiden laughed...

"Have a good day..." Harold said as he walked over to the elevator.

"I can't believe I was so drunk I can't remember what happened..." Mary laughed...

"I don't believe it..." Aiden said as they made their coffee...

"Good morning..." Sonovia yawned...

"Good morning..." Flick breathed as he pulled Sonovia into a kiss...

"Uh uh – I'm not doing that again Flick..." she laughed as she got out of bed and went into the bathroom...

"Guess who?" Flick laughed...

"You need to go?" Sonovia asked as she got up off the toilet...

"I need to go – but I need to cum too..." he laughed...

"What time is check-out?"

"12 o'clock..."

"What time is it now?"

"8 o'clock..."

"C'mon..." Sonovia sighed as she took Flick's hand and pulled him out the bathroom...

"Before we shower and get dressed, I wanna go see Flick and Snow..." Aiden said...

"Oh great – I hope we can get them to spend another night..." Mary said...

"I don't care about that – I wanna know what happened last night..."

"Aiden – I got drunk..." Mary laughed...

"I still wanna talk to them..." he said as they left the room and headed upstairs...

"Oh Flick..."

"Snow... Snow... Snow..."

"Flick... Oh shit... Fuck..."

"Okay – we're here – I hope we caught them before they checked out..." Mary said as they headed down the hallway...

"Flick... Don't stop... I'm cummin'..."

"Cum for me..."

"Huh... Huh... Huh... Huh... Huh..."

"Uuugh! Uuugh! Uuugh! Uuugh! Uuugh!"

"I love you..." she panted...

"I love you too..."

"Let's go get in the shower..."

81

"Okay..."

"Flick? You in there? It's Aiden..." he said as he knocked on the door...

"Maybe they're not in there..." Mary said...

"Flick – I hear somebody knocking..."

"So?"

"Listen – there it goes again..."

"I'll be right back..." Flick sighed as he got out the shower and went to see if anybody was at the door. When he looked out the peep hole, he saw who it was... "Aiden?"

"Yea Flick..."

"We're in the shower – give us a few minutes..."

"Okay – we'll be downstairs – call us when you're ready – I wanna talk to you..."

"Okay..." Flick said as they went down the hall and Flick went back to the bathroom...

"Was somebody at the door?" Sonovia asked...

"Yea – it was Aiden..." he answered as he started washing himself...

"What the fuck? Why are they up here so early?"

"Who knows – he said he wants to talk about last night..."

"Oh shit!"

"What's wrong?"

"Last night somebody saw me pushing Mary in the wheelchair!"

"So what?"

"He asked me if Mary was alright – you think he said something?"

"Baby – you already told the front desk she was drunk – don't worry about it..." he said as he started drying off...

"You right – but why does he wanna talk about last night?"

"Who knows – let's go get dressed so we can get this over with..." he said as he walked into the bedroom and dropped the towel...

"Turn around Baby..." Sonovia commanded...

"Now see... you startin' trouble..." Flick said as he turned around and came towards her...

"I love looking at you naked..." she breathed as she sat down on the bed, grabbed him by his ass, and pushed him in front of her face...

"Snow... they're waiting..."

"Fuck 'em..." she breathed as she took his dick in her mouth...

"Snow... Fuck!" Sonovia loved hearing Flick moan and she began stroking the shaft with her hand while sucking the head of his dick simultaneously... "Snow... Snow... Snow... Oh shit..." Sonovia took his dick all the way in her mouth and when she stroked his balls, he lost it... "I'm cummin'... I'm cummin'... I'm cummin'...

UUUGGGHHH!" Sonovia swallowed and continued sucking his dick softly for a few moments until she was sure nothing would drop off her mouth and just as she stopped sucking Flick pulled her up into his arms and kissed her...

"I wanna get back in this bed and fuck the shit outta you..."

"I'll let you make it up to me later – let's get dressed..."

"Okay – I love you..." he said as they started getting dressed. When they were done, she put on a pot of coffee... "They might still have coffee downstairs..."

"That's okay – I'll drink this – you want some?"

"Sure – make me a cup – I'll call them..." Flick said as he dialed their room... "Aiden? It's Flick... Uh huh – come on up..." After he hung up, Sonovia handed him a cup of coffee... "Thanks Babe..."

"You're welcome..." she said as Aiden knocked on the door...

"Aiden?"

"Yea Flick..." Flick got up and opened the door...

"Good morning – come in..."

"Good morning – good morning Snow..." Aiden said...

"Good morning Flick, good morning Snow..." Mary said...

84

"Good morning guys – did you have breakfast?" Sonovia asked...

"Not yet – my husband wants to talk to you about what happened last night..."

"It was nice until you fell asleep..." Sonovia laughed...

"Did I fall asleep right away?" Aiden asked...

"Naa – we talked about the casino in Queens..." Flick answered...

"We did?"

"Yea – you asked me where I was from – I said Queens – you asked me if they had a casino there – I told you about New Resorts..."

"I don't remember any of that – what the hell's a matter with me?"

"You had a long day yesterday – and a long night – sorry it didn't work out at the tables..."

"I remember that..." Aiden laughed...

"Snow – did you have to push me in a wheelchair?" Mary asked...

"I didn't have to – but you were out of it – I didn't wanna take any chances..."

"Oh my God – was I that bad?"

"No – it wasn't like that – you just fell asleep on the couch – I woke you up – I told you it was time to go to bed, I took you to your room, you got in bed, you went back to sleep..."

"Snow went to sleep on me too..." Flick lied...

"Really?" Aiden asked...

"After I brought you to your room – I came back – she was out!"

"What the hell was in that champagne?" Aiden laughed...

"Snow can't drink wine and champagne together – they both make her sleepy..."

"Oh that's right – we did have wine!" Mary exclaimed...

"I guess Heineken, steak, champagne, and a losing streak didn't do me much good..." Aiden sighed...

"You probably needed the rest – it's a good thing you're staying an extra day..." Flick said...

"I wish you were staying an extra day..." Mary sighed...

"I'm sorry Mary – I can't – I need to get back to work..." Sonovia said...

"You guys wanna go get breakfast?" Aiden asked...

"No thanks – we need to get going..." Flick said...

"Okay – I guess we'll see you next time..." Aiden said as he got up to leave...

"Mary – what's your number?" Sonovia asked as she pulled out her cell phone...

"203-508-2790..." Sonovia put the number in her cell phone and called Mary. Mary looked at her phone... "Is this you?"

"That's me..."

"Okay – I'll save it under Snow..."

"Good – I'll call you later..."

86

"Okay!" Mary exclaimed...

"Okay Flick – nice meeting you – see you soon..."

"Nice meeting you too..." Flick said...

"We'll see ourselves out..." Aiden said as they left. As soon as they left, Flick went over to Sonovia...

"Why the fuck did you give her your phone number?"

"First of all – don't fuckin' talk to me like that!"

"You right Baby – I'm sorry..."

"Second – Aiden already suspects something – we need to act like we cool..."

"You right Baby – I didn't think about that..."

"C'mon – let's check out before they come back with more questions..." she said as she took the bottle of melatonin out the night stand, put it at the bottom of the duffel bag, packed everything into the duffel bag, and left the room...

"Something's not right..." Aiden said as they went back into their room...

"Aiden – what are you getting at?" Mary asked...

"I know something happened last night..."

"Aiden..." Mary breathed as she went over to him and pulled him into a kiss...

"Mary – something h..." Mary kissed him again and this time Aiden relented and held her against him as he kissed her hard...

"I'm hungry..." she breathed...

"What would you like?" he asked, smiling at her seductively...

"You..."

"Coming right up..." he said as he walked her backwards to the bed. Mary fell back and Aiden fell down on top of her, kissed her, went up under her shirt, and began squeezing her breasts as his cell phone rang...

"Don't answer it..." she breathed. Aiden looked at the phone...

"Shit – I need to take this..." he said as he sat up on the bed. Mary got up in a huff, went into the bathroom, and turned on the shower...

"Hello Sean..."

"Aiden – I need more time..."

"I thought I made myself clear..."

"Something happened..."

"I don't wanna hear it..."

"I had your money..."

"Had?"

"I went to the room with them..."

"You're making excuses..."

"I had a glass of champagne..."

"You had a glass of champagne? Are you telling me you don't have my money because you got drunk?"

"I didn't get drunk – I was drugged..."

"I'm hanging up..." Aiden laughed...

"I'm serious – I woke up in my room the next day – with no memory of what happened the night before – and $45,000 transferred out of my account..."

"Where was it transferred?"

"It was transferred to Webster Bank..."

"Did you say you went to their room?"

"That's what I said..."

"Do you remember their names?"

"Flick... and Snow..."

"I'll give you 48 hours..."

"48 hours? That's not enough time – I need a few days!"

"You have 48 hours..." Aiden said as he hung up... "I knew something happened – and now I know why it happened..." Aiden smiled as he got up and went into the bathroom...

"Aiden! You scared me!" Mary exclaimed...

"Don't be scared..." he breathed as he pulled her into a kiss, picked up her leg, and thrust himself up inside her...

"Aiden... Oh God... Aiden... Fuck me..." Mary moaned as she held onto his back...

"Uugh... Uugh... Uugh... Uugh... Uugh..."

"Aiden... Don't stop... Don't stop..."

"Uugh... Uugh... Uugh... Uugh... Uugh..."

"Aiden... I'm cumming! I'm cumming! I'm cumming!"

"Uuugh! Uuugh! Uuugh! Uuugh! Uuugh!"

"Whoever that was..." Mary panted... "I need to thank them..."

"You should be thanking me!!" he growled as he turned her away from him, bent her over, slammed his dick inside her, and began pounding her from behind...

CHAPTER TEN

"Welcome to Webster Bank – how can I help you today?" the teller asked...

"We'd like to make a deposit..." Sonovia answered...

"I can help you with that – I just need your I.D... and your deposit slit..."

"Here you go..." Sonovia said as she put her I.D. and her deposit slip on the counter along with the two checks...

"I see these checks are from Empire Casino..."

"Yes they are..."

"I'm glad you're depositing the checks..."

"Umm... so am I..." Sonovia laughed...

"Oh don't mind me – most people stay at the casino and gamble the money right back..."

"I know..."

"Would you like a receipt?"

"No – just write the account balance on a piece of paper for me..."

"Okay..." she said as she wrote the amount on the paper... "Does that look right to you?"

"Looks fine to me..."

"How long before the money's available?" Flick asked...

"48 hours..." the teller answered...

"Thank you..." Sonovia said as they left the bank... "We have $95,000!" she whispered excitedly...

"I know – I can't believe it!" Flick exclaimed...

"Where are we going next?"

"We could go back to I-Hop – if you want..."

"Naaa – let's go somewhere else – I don't wanna run into Aiden and Mary..."

"C'mon – I know where we can go..." Flick said as he put the address in the Uber and waited...

"I'm gonna like this – right?" Sonovia asked...

"Why would I take you somewhere you won't like?" Flick asked sarcastically as the Uber pulled up...

"You right..." Sonovia said as she got in. Flick went around to the other side and got in...

"Central Plaza Diner?" the Uber driver asked...

"Yes Sir..." Flick answered...

"Okay..." the driver said as he drove off...

"I like diners..." Sonovia said...

"I know..." Flick said as he took her hand...

"Good morning Sam..."

"Good morning Bazil..." Sam said as he closed the door and sat down... "There's $95,000 in the account..."

"Hot Damn!"

"They made a deposit at Webster Bank on Central Avenue in Yonkers..."

"I guess they had a good night at the casino..."

"They had a great night..."

"Did they check out?"

"Yes..."

"They're on the move..."

"I'll keep you posted..."

"Thank you Sam..." Bazil said as he picked up his cell phone...

"Yes Bazil?" Sean answered...

"They have $95,000..."

"That's more than double!"

"Exactly..."

"Are they still in Yonkers?"

"They checked out of the hotel..."

"Shit!"

"That just means they're on the move – they'll settle down somewhere soon – they'll check in – and when they do – I'll let you know..."

"Thank you Bazil..." Bazil hung up his phone, put it down, and just as he was getting ready to start on something else, his phone rang again...

"Hello Conrad..."

"Bazil – I need a favor..."

"What time will you be here?"

"I'll be there in a few minutes..." Conrad said as he hung up. Bazil called Joselyn on the intercom...

"Yes Mr. Osgood?"

"I need to see you..."

"I'll be right there..." Joselyn said as she got up and Beautiee got up with her... "Do you need something?" Joselyn asked...

"I need to find out what my husband wants with you..."

"Okay..." Joselyn laughed as she left to go see Bazil and Beautiee followed... "Yes Mr. Osgood?" Joselyn said as she went into Bazil's office. Bazil smiled as Beautiee came in behind her...

"Joselyn – I'm expecting a Mr. Cox – when he arrives would you escort him to my office?"

"Would you like me to go wait by the entrance?"

"Yes..."

"Okay..." Joselyn said as she left and Beautiee locked the door...

"Mr. Osgood?"

"Yes Mrs. Osgood?" Bazil answered as he got up from behind his desk...

"I need a few moments of your time..." she breathed as she held Bazil against her...

"I can do that..." Bazil breathed as he kissed her. Bazil wrapped his arms around her and kissed her deeply, teasing her lips with his tongue...

"Mmm... you're making me wet..." Bazil continued kissing her as he slid his hand in her pants and began rubbing her clit... "Mmmm..." she moaned as she slid her hand down his pants and grabbed his dick...

"Beautiee..." he moaned...

"I'm cumming..." she moaned. Bazil covered her mouth with his to muffle her sounds... "Mmm... Mmm... Mmm..." Bazil's dick was hard and Beautiee knew he was close to cumming... "Cum in my hand..."

"Mmmph... Mmmph... Mmmph..." Beautiee slid her hand out his pants and licked his cum off her fingers as Bazil was licking her cum off his...

"Mr. Osgood?" Joselyn called out...

"Yes Joselyn?" Bazil answered as they composed themselves...

"Mr. Cox is here..." Beautiee went to the door and unlocked it...

"Hi – I'm Beautiee – Bazil's wife – c'mon Joselyn – let's go get coffee..." she said as she turned Joselyn around and guided her towards the cafeteria...

"Okay..." Joselyn laughed...

"Did I come at a bad time?" Conrad asked...
"Not at all..."
"I need a favor..." he said as he handed Bazil an envelope...
"How can I help you?"
"He's a problem..."
"Is he a serious problem?"
"Yes..."
"Where can I find him?"
"He frequents Mohegan Sun..."
"I'll see what I can do..."
"I appreciate it..."
"I'm not sure what the cost will be yet – I'll know for sure after I take care of it..."
"Thank you Bazil..." Conrad said as he got up to leave...
"We have coffee..." Beautiee said as she came in with two cups of coffee along with Joselyn...
"I'm sorry – I need to..."
"You need to take this coffee..." Beautiee insisted...
"Yes Maam..." Conrad said as he took the coffee...
"Here you go..." Beautiee said as she handed the coffee to Bazil...
"Thank you..."
"You're welcome – Joselyn – I'll take one of those..."

"I was gonna give one to Sam..."

"That's fine – I'll go make myself some coffee..." Beautiee said as she hurried down the hall...

"Here..." Joselyn sighed as she gave Sam a cup of coffee..."

"What's wrong?"

"I had two cups of coffee – Beautiee wanted one – I told her I was giving it to you..."

"Oh so you think she's mad?"

"Yea..."

"She's not mad..."

"Yes she is..."

"Close the door..."

"Okay..." Joselyn said as she went to close the door...

"Come sit down..."

"Okay..." Joselyn said as she went and sat down...

"Guess what?"

"What?"

"Remember the people I told you about?"

"Yea..."

"They just deposited $50,000 into their account..." he whispered...

"Oh my God! How much do they have now?"

"$95,000..."

"What... where..."

"They had a good night at the casino..."

"Did you tell Bazil?"

"Yea..."

"Is he gonna get the money?"

"I didn't ask..."

"Well... I better get back before Beautiee wonders where I'm at..." she sighed as she got up...

"Come here..." Sam commanded. Joselyn went over to Sam and he threw his arms around her and kissed her... "Is that better?"

"Much better..." she sighed as she went back to the office with Beautiee...

"Welcome to central Plaza – table for two?" the hostess asked...

"Yes Maam..." Flick answered...

"Right this way..." the hostess said as they followed her to the table...

"Do you still make breakfast?" Sonovia asked...

"We serve breakfast all day..."

"Oh thank God – can we see your breakfast menu?"

"Sure..." the hostess said as she went to get the menus...

"I'll take those..." the waitress said...

"Thank you – that table over there..."

"Okay..." she said as she went to their table... "Welcome to central Plaza – my name is Delores – I'll give you a moment to look at the menus – would you like coffee?"

"Yes please..." Sonovia exclaimed...

"I'll be right back..." she said...

"Oh Flick look – they have a meat lover's skillet –ham, bacon, sausage over home fries with blended cheese mixed with eggs..."

"Let's get that..." Flick said as the waitress came back with the coffee...

"What can I getcha?" she asked...

"Meat Lover's Skillet!" they both answered in unison...

"Coming right up..." she laughed as she went to place the order...

"Hello Sean..." Bazil answered...

"Bazil – I'm in trouble..."

"You'll be alright..."

"You don't understand..."

"Tell me..."

"He's only giving me 48 hours..."

"Who?"

"Aiden..."

"What's he look like?" Bazil asked...

"He's your complexion, he's about 5 foot 8, he wears diamonds in his ears, and he has a locks in his hair..." Bazil smiled to himself as he listened to Sean describing Conrad's problem...

"You'll have his money... don't worry..."

"He'll kill me if I don't..."

"As soon as they touch down, I'll call you – you have Aiden meet you – he'll get his money –

you'll get your money... and you'll have them right where you want them..."

"I don't give a fuck about them – I just want my money..."

"You should give a fuck about them..."

"Why?"

"They stole from you – you have to have zero tolerance for anyone that crosses you..."

"I don't think I can do that..."

"If you let them get away with this once – who's to say they won't do it again?"

"I never thought of it like that..."

"You have to think of it like that – you don't have a choice..."

"Thank you Bazil..."

"You're welcome..." Bazil said as he hung up...

CHAPTER ELEVEN

"Oh my God!" Mary exclaimed as she looked at her laptop...

"What's wrong?" Aiden asked...

"You're not going to believe this..." she said as she turned her laptop around so Aiden could see it...

"Oh wow..."

"Can you believe it? She's an author! I could've gotten her autograph! I wonder why she didn't tell me..."

"She was probably relieved you didn't know who she really was..."

"Really?"

"Yea – once you're famous you don't really know if people want to know you for you or if they want to get close to you to see what you can do for them..."

"I'm glad we got to know her without knowing she's an author – I really like her..."

"I like her too..."

"I'm gonna buy her books right now!" Mary exclaimed...

"Easy Mary – your balance is high enough on amazon as it is..." Aiden laughed...

"You never complain when I'm buying toys for you..." she laughed as she started downloading books to her kindle...

"We need to get ready – it's almost time to check out..."

"Are we going home?"

"Not yet..."

"Aiden..." she sighed...

"I know... but I need to make some money..."

"That's what you always say..."

"This is the last time... I promise..."

"You always say that too..."

"Mary..." he sighed as he sat on the bed... "I need to tell you something..."

"What's wrong?"

"I didn't just come here to gamble..."

"Oh my God – how much?"

"How much what?"

"How much do you owe?"

"$45,000..."

"Oh Aiden..." she sighed...

"I was expecting a payment... he doesn't have my money..."

"Are we going to lose everything?"

"Mary... listen to me..." he said as he took her hands in his... "We have the rental properties, we have the shopping centers, and our mortgage is paid in full..."

"Our mortgage is paid? Oh my God! When?"

"Last month..."

"Oh Aiden!" Mary exclaimed as she kissed him... "Why didn't you tell me?"

"I was going to surprise you..."

"But we still can't go home..."

"I'd like to see if I can recoup my losses..."

"That's not the only reason..."

"I gave him another 48 hours to come up with my money..."

"What if he doesn't have it?"

"We're going home whether he has it or not..." he answered as he lay her down on the bed, got on top of her, and started kissing her...

"Where are we going now?" Sonovia asked...

"I wanna go to Mohegan Sun... but we can't..." Flick answered...

"Why can't we?"

"They don't have a Webster Bank up there..."

"Why do we need to go to Webster Bank up there? Why can't we go back where we made the deposit?"

"It's better to leave the casino after you hit the jackpot – especially when you hit a big one – they start tryin' to comp you free rooms, free drinks, free food – the longer you stay, the better the chance of you giving them back their money..."

"Oh hell no – we not doin' that..."

"Exactly..."

"So where are we goin'?"

"We gotta go to Trumbull..."

"Naa... I don't like the Marriott..."

"You wanna go back to the Hyatt?"

"Naa..."

"You wanna go home?"

"Naa – if we go home then we have to go to the bank on Lexington – I don't wanna walk around New York with a bag full of cash..."

"I don't either..."

"Don't they have a branch in Bridgeport?"

"Yea..."

"Why don't we just get a room at the Holiday Inn and stay there until the money clears?"

"You sure that's what you want?"

"Yea – we can go out later if we want, we can go to happy hour at Park City Grill, we can go swimming..."

"That's right – you did bring your bathing suit..."

"I did..." she said as she smiled at him mischievously...

104

"Joselyn?"

"Yes Sam?"

"Could you come in here a minute?"

"I'll be right there..." she said as she got up. Joselyn looked back at Beautiee and Beautiee had her head in the computer so she went to Sam's office and closed the door... "Hey..." she sighed...

"You still think Beautiee's mad at you?"

"Yea..."

"Did she say something?"

"She hasn't said anything..."

"So she's just sitting at her desk – and she's not saying anything?"

"She's on her computer..."

"She's not mad at you – she's into one of her books..."

"I hope you're right..." she sighed...

"Come here..." Sam said as he got up and came out from behind his desk...

"Yes Sam?" she sighed as she put her arms around his neck...

"Another deposit just hit the account..."

"How much was this one?"

"$30,000..."

"How do they do that?"

"This one came from amazon..."

"As much money as I spend – I need amazon to pay me $30,000..." Joselyn laughed...

"You need to stop shopping at amazon..."

"Why would I do that when everything I buy makes you happy?" she breathed as she kissed him...

"Joselyn?"

"Yes Beautiee?"

"I need to see you when you get a chance..."

"I'll see you later..." she sighed...

"I need to go talk to Bazil..." Sam said as he went to Bazil's office...

"Bazil – I need to talk to you..." Sam said as he closed the door...

"What's wrong?"

"Nothing – I just came to give you an update..."

"Tell me..."

"An electronic deposit just hit the account..."

"Damn – they work fast..."

"It was from amazon..."

"Really? How much?"

"$30,000..."

"She's an author..."

"You think so?"

"I know so – amazon doesn't pay their employees an annual salary all at once..." Bazil laughed...

"Yes Beautiee?"

"Here – read this – tell me what you think..." Beautiee said as she guided Joselyn to her desk and sat her in front of the laptop...

"Ooohhh... I like this already..." Joselyn exclaimed as she kept reading. Beautiee watched intently and smiled as Joselyn's eyes got really big... "Is this a new book?"

"Yea..."

"I like it..."

"What do you think of the title?"

"The Ultimate Con... I like it..."

"Thanks..." Beautiee smiled...

"I'm going to lunch with Sam..." Joselyn said as she got up...

"Okay – see you later..."

"We're here..." the Uber driver said as they pulled up to the Holiday Inn...

"Thank you..." Flick said as he opened the door and got out. When he went to open the door for Sonovia, she was already out... "Babe – why didn't you let me open the door for you?"

"I was tired of sitting..."

"C'mon – let's go inside..." Flick said as he took her hand and walked her inside...

"Welcome to the Holiday Inn – are you checking in?" the concierge clerk asked...

"Yes we are..." Sonovia answered...

"Name please?"

"Sonovia Alexander..."

"Oh my God – can I have your autograph?"

"You know who I am?"

"I have your book right here!" she gushed as she pulled the book out her purse...

"From The Projects To A Rich Man's Mansion – that's one of my favorites..."

"Is everything okay?" the manager asked as he came over...

"Everything's fine..." Sonovia answered...

"Okay – just checking..." he said as he walked away...

"I swear – he gets on my fucking nerves..." the clerk sighed...

"He does that all the time?"

"He wants us to be fuckin' robots – don't talk – don't socialize..."

"Le'me give you my autograph..." Sonovia said as she signed the book...

"Thank you so much – I can't wait to..."

"Uh uh – please don't..."

"I understand – can I get a picture with you though?"

"Sure – Flick – help her out..." Sonovia said as she posed with the clerk and the clerk gave Flick her cell phone...

"Thank you!" she gushed...

"You're welcome..."

"Why isn't she checked in yet?" the manager snapped...

"Excuse me – what is your name?" Sonovia asked...

"I'm Mr. Outtaway..."

"I'm Sonovia Alexander – CEO of Sonovia Alexander Presents..."

"That's nice – but that doesn't explain why you're still not check in..."

"I was asking your clerk about holding an event at this hotel..."

"Oh... I see... I'd be happy to discuss that with you..."

"Naa – I'ma look somewhere else – I don't like how you treat your employees – matter of fact – I don't even wanna stay here..."

"Ms. Alexander – wait – please reconsider – tell you what – I'll comp you the room – Virginia – please comp them their room..."

"That's nice – I appreciate it – but you need to apologize to your employee..."

"Virginia – I apologize..."

"Apology accepted..."

"Enjoy your stay – here's my card..." he said as he handed his card to her...

"Thank you..." Sonovia said...

"Have a good evening..." he said as he walked away...

"Oh my God! Thank you!" Virginia exclaimed...

"You're welcome – don't post that picture until we check out – okay?"

"Okay!" she exclaimed as she checked them in... "I gave you a room on the 3rd floor so you'll be near the pool..." she said as she handed Sonovia the room keys...

"Thank you Virginia..."

"Oh no – thank you!"

"What room are we in Babe?" Flick asked as they went towards the elevator...

"We're in room 325..." she answered as they got in the elevator and went up to their room...

"Hang on a minute..." Sam said as he stopped by Bazil's office...

"What now?" Joselyn asked...

"I need to tell Bazil something..." Sam said as he went into Bazil's office...

"Yes Sam?"

"They just check into the Holiday Inn in Bridgeport..."

"Any change in the account?"

"No..."

"Thank you Sam..."

"You're welcome – I'm out to lunch – call me if you need me...

"I'll try not to..." Bazil laughed...

"We good now?" Joselyn asked...

"We're great..." Sam sighed as he wrapped his arm around her, pulled her close to him, and walked her to the car...

"Hello Bazil..."

"They just check into the Holiday Inn at Bridgeport..."

"Thank you Bazil – I'm on my way..."

"Don't do anything until they get the money..."

"I won't..." Sean said as he hung up...

"I'ma fuck you up!" Sonovia exclaimed as Flick pushed her into the pool. Flick jumped in the water, swam over to her, and kissed her... "This water has chlorine in it – you should 'a let me wrap my hair..."

"Baby – when we get home – I'll get your hair done..." he breathed as he kissed her... "Your nails done..." he breathed as he kissed her again... "Your feet done..." he breathed as he kissed her again... "And anything else you want done..."

"Oh shit Flick – look!" Sonovia exclaimed as she pointed to the entrance...

"What's wrong?" Flick asked just as Sean moved away from the door...

"I thought I saw Sean..."

"You trippin' – how would he know where we are anyway?"

"You right... I'm trippin'..." she sighed as Flick held his arms under her and she began floating...

"You goin' in man?" somebody asked, interrupting Sean...

"Umm... No... Sorry..." he said as he left the pool area and went back to his room...

CHAPTER TWELVE

"Good morning..." Flick breathed as he kissed Sonovia awake...

"Good morning... sorry I went to sleep on you last night..."

"That's okay – you can make it up to me now if you want..." he breathed as he kissed her again...

"I'm sorry – I just wanna get this money and get outta here..." she sighed...

"Okay..." he sighed as he got up...

"Flick – where you goin'?"

"I'm goin' to get in the shower..."

"I'm comin' with you..."

"You know what's gonna happen when you come in here – right?"

"Yes Flick..." she laughed...

"Good morning Mr. Stewart – what can we get you?"

"I'll have the buffet..."

"Would you like coffee?"

"Yes please..." he answered as he got up and went over to the buffet...

"Welcome to Mohegan Sun – are you here to check in?"

"Yes we are..." Aiden sighed...

"Name please?"

"Aiden Holloway..."

"Mr. Holloway – I see you're booked for the Sky Tower..."

"The Sky Tower?! Oh Aiden!" Mary exclaimed...

"Mr. Holloway, you're all set..." the clerk said as she handed him the room keys..."

"Thank you..." he smiled as he took Mary by the hand and escorted her to the elevator..."

"What room are we in?" Mary asked...

"We're in room 640..." Aiden answered as they got on the elevator...

"Damn – I wish I could fuck you like this at home..." Flick said as he dried off...

"Why can't you?"

"Cause we have neighbors..."

"I'on give a fuck!" Sonovia laughed...

"Okay – I'ma remember that..." Flick laughed as they went into the bedroom and got dressed...

"Would you like anything else?" the waitress asked...

"No thank you – I'll just take the check..."

"Would you like it charged to the room?"

"Yes..."

"Okay – sign here and we'll take care of it..." she said as she placed the bill on the table. Sean signed the check, finished his coffee, and got up...

"Have a nice day..."

"Same to you..." Sean said as he left the dining area. When he got to his room, he stripped, went straight to the shower, turned it on, and got in... "I'll see you soon Snow..." he breathed as he started washing himself...

"What can I get you?" the waitress asked...

"We'll have the buffet..." Sonovia answered...

"Ms. Alexander – your breakfast has been comped – enjoy..."

"Thank you..." Sonovia said as the waitress walked away...

"Well then – let me see what they have at the buffet..." Flick said as he got up...

"I hope they have coffee over there..." Sonovia said as she got up. The waitress heard

Sonovia, went to get a pot of coffee, and placed it on the table...

"Aiden... Oh Aiden... Fuck me..."

"Is this how you like it?"

"I love it... Oh God... Yeesss..."

"Whose pussy is this?!"

"Yours Aiden... Yours!"

"Damn right it's mine!" he growled as he spread her legs and fucked her harder...

"Aiden... Aiden... I'm cumming... I'm cumming..."

"Uuugh! Uuugh! Uuugh! Uuugh! Uuuggghhh!"

"Oh Aiden..." Mary panted...

"Yeesss..." Aiden breathed as he kissed her...

"I don't know what's gotten into you... but I love it..."

"I love you too..." he breathed as they went for round two..."

"What time is it?" Sonovia asked...

"It's just about 9..."

"Good – we can go to the room, check out, and go to the bank..."

"Let's make sure they can give us the money before we check out..."

"Okay – we'll go over there now – if they say we have to wait – we'll come back to the room..."

"Okay – let's go..." Flick said as they got up and left the hotel...

"Well, well, well... I see you're on your way to get my money..." Sean said as he followed them. When he got to the bank, Sean looked around and didn't see them so he went up to the counter and pretended to fill out a deposit slip, and that's when he noticed them walking towards the door with the bank manager. They were talking, but Sean couldn't make out what they were saying...

"I'm glad I listened to you..." Sonovia said...
"I'm glad too..." Flick said...
"What are we gonna do now?"
"Let's go back to the room and try to relax..."
"Okay..."

"Hmmm... I see you didn't get my money yet..." Sean said as he followed them. Sean waited for them to enter the hotel. When they got on the elevator, he went inside, got on the elevator, got off the elevator, and went to room 323 – right next door to Flick and Snow...

"Come here..." Flick said as he pulled Sonovia into a kiss...
"Flick... I..."

116

"Ssshhh..." he breathed as he kissed her again. Sonovia didn't speak as he took her hand and led her to the bed. Flick lay down on the bed, patted the bed for her to lie down beside him, and she fell asleep as soon as she snuggled up underneath him...

"Yes Bazil?" Sean answered...
"How's everything going?"
"They just left the bank..."
"Did they get your money?"
"No..."
"Where are they now?"
"They're back in their room..."
"Let me know when they move again..."
"I will..." Sean said as he hung up...

"Are you hungry?" Aiden asked...
"I'm hungry..." Mary breathed...
"What would you like?"
"I'd like to go to the buffet..."
"Is it open?"
"I believe it is..."
"We'll go to the buffet – if it's not open – we'll find something open..." Aiden said as he started to get up but Mary pulled him back down... "I thought you said you were hungry?"

"I am..." she breathed as she pulled him down on top of her, spread her legs, and pulled him into a kiss...

117

"Oh shit – what time is it?" Sonovia exclaimed as she sat up...

"It's 11 o'clock..."

"Flick – why didn't you wake me up?"

"I wasn't gonna let you sleep past check out..." he said as they got up...

"Okay – let's check out now – we can wait at the bank..." she said as they put everything in the bag, left the room, and dropped the room keys in the key box...

"Ms. Alexander – come with me..." the bank manager said as he held the door open for them. Flick and Sonovia followed the bank manager into his office and sat down. The manager came in and closed the door... "We prefer to do large transactions in private..." he explained...

"I appreciate that..." Sonovia said. The manager began placing stacks of bills on the table and Flick started counting the money...

"I hope you have a bag for this..." the manager laughed...

"We do..." Flick laughed as he put the money in the bag...

"You have $25,000 left in your account..."

"Thank you..." Sonovia said as she got up...

"You're welcome..." the manager said as he got up... "Have a nice day..."

"You too..." Flick said as they left the bank...

"The Uber will be here in 5 minutes..." Flick said...

"Good – I can't wait to get to Mohegan Sun..."

"I can't either..." Flick sighed...

"Oh shit!" Sean exclaimed as he jumped up... "It's 12 o'clock – shit, shit, shit!" he exclaimed as he ran and opened his door. When he saw housekeeping in their room, he went inside...

"Did you leave something in here?" she asked...

"I was looking for my friends..."

"They checked out an hour ago..."

"Thank you..." Sean said as he went back to his room and called Bazil...

"Yes Sean..."

"I fucked up..."

"What do you mean?"

"They're gone..."

"They're gone?"

"They checked out about an hour ago..."

"How did they get by you?"

"I fell asleep..." Sean sighed...

"Stay where you are..."

"But Bazil..."

"Stay where you are until you hear from me..." Bazil commanded as he hung up...

"Sam..."

"Yes Bazil?"

"Could you come in here for a minute?"

"Sure..." Bazil waited for Sam to come in...

"Close the door..." Bazil sighed...

"What's wrong?"

"My friend's a fuckin' idiot!" Bazil exclaimed...

"What'd he do?"

"I told him where they were – I told him don't do anything until they get his money – he had a room right next door to them – and he falls asleep!"

"They checked out?"

"They checked out..." Bazil sighed...

"We'll get 'em..."

"We don't know where they are!"

"They have $100,000 cash – they're not going to carry that money around with them – they're gonna check into a hotel – or they're gonna go home..."

"You're right..."

"I gotchu Bazil – don't worry..."

"Thank you Sam..."

120

CHAPTER THIRTEEN

"I guess the buffet is open..." Mary laughed as they got online...

"I hope you're not too hungry..." Aiden sighed... "We might be here for a while..."

"I don't mind..." Mary sighed...

"Let's see how you feel after being on line for 30 minutes..." the lady in front of her said...

"30 minutes?" Mary repeated...

"Almost 45 now..." the lady answered...

"Why don't we get off this line and go to Ballo? It's an Italian restaurant..." Aiden suggested...

"That line is just as long as this one..." the lady answered as if Aiden was talking to her...

"Mary? What do you think?"

"I think I'd like some Italian food..."

"Okay – c'mon..." Aiden said as he took Mary by the hand...

"Good luck!" the lady laughed...

"Welcome to Ballo – there's a 30-minute wait for a table..." the hostess said...

"That's fine..." Aiden said...

"Name please?"

"Aiden..."

"May I have your phone number?"

"You want my phone number?"

"Yes – we'll text you when your table is ready..."

"Okay – 475-808-9234..."

"Thank you – we'll see you soon..."

"C'mon Aiden – I see a progressive Wheel of Fortune I wanna play!" Mary exclaimed as she pulled Aiden by the hand...

"Easy Mary – you're still new at this..." he laughed...

"Don't worry – I remember what Snow told me..." she explained as she sat down...

"What's that?" Aiden asked as she put a $20 bill in the machine...

"Snow said start with $10 - $20 – see how I do..." she answered as she pulled the lever. They both watched the wheel spin... "Oh shoot... oh well..." she sighed as she placed another bet and watched the wheel spin... "Aiden – look!" she exclaimed as she watched the bonus wheel spin...

"Did you just win $20,000?"

"I did!"

"Congratulations..."

"Thank you!" Mary exclaimed as she cashed out...

"What are you doing?"

"I'm doing what Snow told me..." Mary sighed as she cashed out and put the ticket in her purse...

"What's wrong?"

"I wish she was here..."

"You'll see her again..."

"I know..."

"You have her phone number – you can always give her a call..." Aiden said as he took her by the hand...

"Where are we going now?"

"To eat – our table is ready..."

"Welcome to Mohegan Sun – are you here to check in?"

"Yes Maam..." Flick answered...

"Name please?"

"Sonovia Alexander..." Sonovia answered...

"Welcome back Ms. Alexander – I see you're booked for the Sky Tower..."

"Thank you – yes we are..."

"You're all set..." the concierge clerk said as she handed Sonovia the room keys...

"Thank you..." Sonovia said as she took the keys from her...

"What room are we in this time?" flick asked...

"We're in room 642..."

"C'mon – I can't wait to get in our room..." Flick said as he took Sonovia's hand and pulled her to the elevator...

"Yes Sam?" Bazil asked as Sam came into his office and closed the door...

"They just checked into the Sky tower at Mohegan Sun..."

"Thank you Sam..."

"I got their room number too – they're in room 642..."

"Thank you Sam..." Bazil said as he jumped up from behind his desk... "I gotta run – if Beautiee asks where I am – tell her I had to leave and I'll see her later!" he exclaimed as he ran past Sam and left. As soon as he got in the car, he called Mike...

"Yes Mr. Osgood?"

"I need you to meet me at my house..."

"Yes Sir Mr. Osgood..." Mike said as he hung up...

"Yes Bazil?" Sean answered...

"They just checked into Mohegan Sun..."

"Thank you Bazil..."

"They're staying in the Sky Tower – Room 642..."

"Thank you Bazil – I'm on my way..."

"Make sure you keep in touch..." Bazil said as he hung up and drove out the parking lot. As soon as Bazil got home, he parked, hurried out the car, ran into the house, and ran upstairs to the bedroom. Bazil searched through the nightstand for a pen and some paper, and wrote Beautiee the following:

"Beautiee, I'm sorry I had to run out of the office today without saying goodbye – I won't be home until late – I'll make it up to you – I love you – see you tonight, love Bazil..." Bazil left the note on the nightstand hurried back downstairs, and when he got outside, Mike was waiting for him...

"Hello Mr. Osgood – where to?"

"Mohegan Sun..."

"Going to win some money?"

"Absolutely..."

"Yes Sir..." Mike said as he drove off...

"Welcome to Ballo – would you like some garlic bread to start?" the waitress asked...

"Yes please..." Mary answered...

"Can I get you something to drink?"

"I'll have a Tequila Pomegranate Sour!" Mary exclaimed...

"What can I get you?" the waitress asked as she turned to Aiden...

"I'll have a Guinness..."

125

"I'll be back..." the waitress said as she went to get the garlic bread and drinks...

"Ooohhh... I see what I want..." Mary exclaimed...

"What's that?" Aiden asked...

"Toagliatelle..."

"Shrimp scampi... looks good..."

"What are you having Dear?"

"I'm going to have the Double R Ranch Prime New York Strip..."

"That sounds good too..." Mary sighed...

"Have you decided?" the waitress asked as she walked up to the table...

"We have..." Aiden answered...

"What'll it be?"

"Tagliatelle and Double R Ranch Prime New York Strip..."

"How would you like your steak?"

"Well done..."

"Would you like any appetizers?"

"No..."

"Would you like any salad?"

"No..."

"Okay – I'll be back..."

"We did it!" Flick exclaimed as he dropped the bags on the floor, picked Sonovia up off the floor, and spun her around...

"I can't believe it!" she exclaimed...

126

"And now that we're here..." he said as he put her back down on the floor and pulled her into a kiss...

"Yes Flick..." she breathed as he walked her back towards the bed and pushed her down on it...

"I can give you what I owe you..." he breathed as he climbed up on the bed, unbuttoned her jeans, and unzipped them... "Let me..." he breathed as he moved her hands, pulled her jeans down to her ankles, and snatched them off. He surprised her when he picked up the thong in his teeth and pulled it down...

"Ooohhh... okay!" Flick pulled the thong off her ankles, grabbed them, and snatched her legs open. When Sonovia gasped, he smiled at her mischievously...

"And now..." he breathed as he lay down between her legs... "It's time for dessert..." he growled as he put his head between her legs and began shaking his head back and forth on her lips. Sonovia bust out laughing as Flick expected she would but when he spread her lips and flicked his tongue on her clit, she went from laughing to moaning...

"Ooohhh... Ooohhh... Ooohhh..." her moaning was music to his ears as he began to satisfy his taste buds on her juices... "Flick... Oh shit..." Flick stopped flicking his tongue on her clit and began licking up and down her pussy as he grabbed her ass and lifted her up off the bed...

127

Ooohhh... Ooohhh... Ooohhh..." Sonovia was dripping and when Flick stuck his tongue in her pussy while rubbing his nose against her clit, she started trembling... "Flick... Yessss... Don't stop..." Flick saved the best for last when he put her back down on the bed, put a finger in her ass, a finger in her pussy, and massaged her g-spot with his fingers while simultaneously sucking her clit... "FFLLIICCKK! OH GOD! FFUUCCKK! I'M CCUUMMIINNGG!" Sonovia came so hard her legs shook around Flick's head...

"Mmmm..." he moaned as he continued licking and sucking...

"Shit..." she panted... "I can't move..."

"Let me help you with that..." Flick said as he got up and lifted her up...

"Damn..." she breathed as she kissed him hard...

"You hungry?"

"Umm... Yea..."

"C'mon – we'll go have dinner..." he said as he picked up her thong and put it back on her legs. Sonovia sat there as he put her jeans back on her legs and when he stood her up, he pulled them up around her waist and kissed her again...

"Le'me put these boots on so we can hurry up and get outta here..." she said as she put on her boots...

"You in a hurry?"

"I'm in a hurry to get down there... so we can get back in here..."

"Ooohhh... Okay..."

"Make sure you put the money in the safe..."

"Le'me do that right now..." Flick said as he picked up the bag, checked it for the money, and put it in the safe...

"What's the combination?" Sonovia asked as they left the room and closed the door...

"Your measurements..." he answered as he took her hand and led her to the elevator...

"I'm sorry..." Aiden said as he looked at his cell phone...

"Aiden – let it go to voice mail..." Mary pleaded as she touched his hand...

"I'm sorry – I can't..." he said as he answered his phone... "This is Aiden..."

"You'll get your money later tonight..." Sean said...

"Is that right?"

"How long will it take you to get to Mohegan Sun?"

"I'm already here..." Aiden answered as he smiled...

"I'll text you when I arrive..." Sean said as he hung up...

"I'm glad you took that call..." Mary said...

"Really?"

"Yes..."

"Why?"

"You're smiling..." Aiden didn't say anything – he just continued eating... "Would you like to share what or who has you smiling like that?"

"Are you jealous?" Aiden laughed...

"I'm not jealous... I'm curious..."

"I'm getting paid tonight..."

"Oh Aiden – that's wonderful!"

"Yes it is..." Aiden agreed...

"How's everything?" the waitress asked as she came over...

"Wonderful..." Aiden sighed...

"Would you like anything else?"

"I'd like a refill for my wife as well as myself..."

"Okay..." the waitress said as she left...

"Aiden - what are you doing? Remember the champagne?"

"I'm getting you drunk so I can take you back to bed and have my way with you..." Aiden answered, smiling at her mischievously...

"Oh Aiden..." Mary gushed as the waitress put the check on the table. Aiden signed the check, put their room number on it, got up from the table, helped Mary up, and they left the restaurant...

CHAPTER FOURTEEN

"Welcome to Ballo – there's a 30-minute wait for a table..." the hostess said...

"That's fine..." Sonovia said...

"Name please?"

"Sonovia..."

"May I have your phone number?"

"You want my phone number?"

"Yes – we'll text you when your table is ready..."

"Okay – 718—545-9281..."

"Thank you – we'll see you soon..."

"We might as well walk around and see if I wanna play a game or two..." Sonovia said...

"Uh uh – you said you were in a hurry to get down here so we could get back up there..." Flick laughed...

"I know what I said!" she laughed as she pulled Flick towards the progressive triple seven machines...

"Yes Sean..." Bazil answered...

"I'm here..."

"Good – make sure you go straight to the Sky Tower..."

"I got it – room 642..." Sean said as he hung up...

"How much longer until we get there Mike?"

"We should be there in another 15 minutes..."

Sean parked his car and got out... "I can't believe I was able to find parking on this level..." he said out loud as he set the alarm on the car and walked towards the elevator. When he got in the elevator he looked for the door that led to the hotel, went through the door, and walked down the corridor... "Here we are – room 642..." he said out loud. Sean listened at the door and didn't hear any noise...

"May I help you?" the cleaning lady asked...

"I'm so embarrassed – I left my room key inside – I came back to get it but my wife left the room – she's in the casino somewhere – I tried to call her but she probably has her phone in her pocket..." he lied...

"I'm not supposed to do this..." she said as she used her key to open the door... "But I won't tell if you don't..."

"Thank you so much..." he said as he handed her a $20 bill... "I really appreciate it..."

"You're welcome..." she said as she put the $20 bill in her pocket and went down the corridor to another room...

"Yes Sean..." Bazil answered...

"I'm in the room..."

"Why are you calling me?"

"They're not here... so I'm going to wait..."

"Okay – call me and let me know when they get there..." Bazil said as he hung up...

"We're here Mr. Osgood..."

"Thanks Mike – I'm going to be a while..."

"I get paid by the hour..." Mike laughed as Bazil got out and went inside the casino. Bazil found a bar near the hotel, found a comfortable seat, and watched the game as he waited for Sean to call him...

"Next!" the cashier called out. Mary went up to the window and placed her ticket and I.D. on the counter...

"Congratulations..."

"Thank you..."

"How would you like it?"

"I'd like $1,000 cash and the rest in a check..."

"It'll be a few minutes... I need to get the manager's approval for checks over $10,000..."

"Okay..." Aiden and Mary waited for a few moments...

"Ms. Holloway – I need you to come with me..." an officer said as he approached...

"Is there a problem?"

"Not at all – I just need to escort you inside so you can sign for your check..."

"Can my husband come with me?"

"I'm sorry – we only escort the person signing the check – it'll just be a moment..." he said as he guided her towards the door and they went inside...

"Congratulations Ms. Holloway..." the manager said...

"Thank you..."

"Just sign here and you're all set..." the manager said as he handed her a paper to sign. Mary signed the paper and the manager handed her the check...

"Thank you..." she said as she put the check in her purse...

"Okay – let's get you back to your husband..." the officer said as he escorted her back out by the cashier...

"Everything okay?" Aiden asked...

"I think... I'm drunk..." Mary laughed...

"You're not drunk... you're just a little tipsy..." Aiden laughed...

"Are you still going to have your way with me?" she asked as Aiden took her by the hand...

"Absolutely..." he answered, smiling at her mischievously. Mary smiled as they walked to the elevator and got in. As soon as the doors closed, Aiden was all over Mary...

"Aiden..." she breathed...

"I can't wait to get you back in bed..." he breathed as the elevator doors opened. Mary was all smiles as he took her hand, walked her down the corridor to their room, and opened the door. As soon as they got inside, he picked Mary up in his arms, carried her to the bed, picked up where he left off in the elevator, and began removing her clothes...

"Oh shoot – I'll come back and play later – our table's ready..." Sonovia laughed as she got up...

"C'mon..." Flick said as he took her hand and they went back to the restaurant...

"Hi – we received a text that our table was ready..." Sonovia said...

"Name please?"

"Sonovia..."

"Right this way..." the hostess said as she led them to a booth and they sat down...

"Welcome to Ballo – would you like some garlic bread to start?" the waitress asked...

"Naa..." Sonovia answered...

"Can I get you something to drink?"

"I'll have a Tequila Pomegranate Sour..."

"What can I get you?" the waitress asked as she turned to Flick...

"I'll have a Nero Manhattan..."

"I'll be back..." the waitress said as she went to get the drinks...

"Ooohhh... I see what I want..." Sonovia exclaimed...

"What's that?" Flick asked...

"Point Judith Calamari Fritti..."

"What the hell is that?" Flick laughed...

"Calamari – squid – octopus..."

"If that's what you want..." Fick laughed...

"What are you having?"

"I'ma get the chicken parmigiana..."

"I'ma get the linguini with crab..."

"Have you decided?" the waitress asked as she walked up to the table...

"She wants that calamari fritti" Flick said as he put his hand and then put up his pinky...

"Would you like an appetizer as well?"

"No thank you..."

"What else would you like?"

"Chicken parmigiana and linguini with crab..."

"Would you like any salads?"

"I don't want a salad – you want a salad Babe?" Flick asked...

"No..."

"Okay – I'll be back..." the waitress said as she went to place the order...

136

"Aiden... Aiden... Aiden..." Mary moaned...

"Is that... Naa..." Sean laughed...

"Uugh! Uuugh! Uuugh!"

"Aiden... Don't Stop... Aiden..."

"I'm just getting started..." Aiden growled...

"Oh my God! That is Aiden!" Sean laughed...

"Bang... Bang... Bang..." went the head board as Aiden and Mary continued...

"This has got to be a fucking joke!" Sean laughed...

"That's it Mary... Suck it..."

"Oohhh... Now we're talkin'..." Sean said as he got up and went over to the wall...

"Mary... Oh shit... Fuck... I'm cumming... Uuugh! Uuugh! Uuugh! Uuuggghhhh!"

"Okay Aiden..." Sean said as he continued to listen...

"Sit on my face..."Aiden said...

"Oh shit!" Sean exclaimed...

"Aiden... Aiden... Haa... Haa... Haa... Don't stop...Oh God... AAAIIIDDDEEENNN!"

"My man!" Sean exclaimed...

"Yes Sean..." Bazil answered...

"You're not going to believe this..." Sean laughed...

"What..."

"I'm sitting here listening to Aiden and his wife fucking..."

137

"What?"

"Aiden and his wife are in the next room..."

"Don't fuck this up Sean..."

"I'm not!"

"When they come back – you get the money – you come downstairs – you get me – you give the man his money – and then you get the fuck outta here!"

"Okay, okay..."

"I'm serous!"

"I know – shoot – it's quiet – I'll call you when I'm on my way downstairs...

"How's everything?" the waitress asked as she came over...

"Delicious..." Flick said...

"Would you like anything else?"

"I'd like another one of these..." Sonovia said...

"I'd like another drink too..." Flick said...

"Okay – I'll be right back..." the waitress said as she went to get their drinks...

"Here ya go..." the waitress said as she came back with their drinks and put them on the table along with their check... "Would you like to charge this to your room?"

"Yes Maam..." Flick answered...

"That's fine – just sign the check, put your room number, and you'll be all set..." she said as she went to take care of another table. Flick and

Sonovia continued to sit there for a few moments as they finished their drinks...

"You ready?" he asked...

"Yea... I'm ready..." Sonovia answered, smiling mischievously...

"You startin' trouble again – okay..." Flick said as he signed the check, put their room number on it, got up from the table, helped Sonovia up, and they left the restaurant. As soon as they got in the elevator, Flick was all over Sonovia...

"Stop playin' Flick – I'll drop down and suck your dick right here – I'on give a fuck!"

"You goin' suck my dick – okay..." Flick said as he started to open his pants and the elevator doors opened...

"Good evening..." the man said...

"Good evening..." Flick and Sonovia said. Flick and Sonovia looked at each other and smiled. Neither one of them said anything until the man got off the elevator...

"What was that you said you was gonna do?" Flick asked...

"Naa... that was too close..." she laughed as the doors opened again and they got off the elevator. They walked down the corridor to their room, opened the door, and Flick turned on the light...

CHAPTER FIFTEEN

"Beautiful Snow..." Sean breathed...

"Sean?!" Flick exclaimed...

"You should've killed me..."

"What..."

"What am I doing here? Do you really need me to answer that?" he asked as he got up out the chair, walked over to Sonovia, and put his arm around her...

"Take your hands off my wife!" Flick demanded...

"Shut the fuck up!" Sean exclaimed as he reached behind his back and pulled a 9 millimeter out his pants...

"I'll do whatever you want – just don't hurt my wife..." Flick pleaded...

"That's better..." Sean said as he pulled Sonovia closer to him and kissed her... "Now...

140

here's what I want you to do..." he breathed in Sonovia's ear... "I want you to go in the bathroom... I want you to put on that red garter outfit... and I want you to come back out here..."

"Okay..." Sonovia said as she nodded her head...

"Don't make me have to come get you..."

"I won't..." she said as she went into the bathroom...

"Flick... I'm going to ask you a question..."

"Your money's in the safe..."

"Let's go get it..." Sean said as he got up from the bed and went towards the closet...

"You don't have to have a gun in my back – I'll do what you want..." Flick said as he unlocked the safe...

"You and I both know I can't trust you..."

"I'll do whatever you want – just don't hurt my wife..." Flick said as he opened the safe...

"Take out the duffel bag..." Flick did as he was told... "Put it over there..." Flick took the bag out the closet and put it on the floor by the duffel bag with the clothes... "Snow?" he called...

"I'm coming..." she said as she came out...

"You look stunning..." he breathed as he looked her up and down. He could see she was embarrassed and ashamed and he was enjoying it... "Go over there and make us a drink – but this time, I want you to give Flick the glass you gave me..."

"Okay..." Sonovia said as she walked in front of him...

"They have to be back by now..." Bazil said out loud as he took out his cell phone and sent the following text, "What's going on? I'm at the bar – hit me back..."

"Damn you're sexy..." Sean breathed. Flick didn't take his eyes off Sean. Sean was watching Sonovia intently as she poured the champagne into the glasses... "Don't forget the special ingredient..." Sean said as he took the bottle of melatonin out the nightstand drawer and shook it. Sonovia walked over to Sean and stood in front of him... "My God – you're gorgeous..." he breathed as he put the gun down beside him and ran his hands up her hips. Flick watched intently but didn't move. Unfortunately for him, he was too far away to get his hands on the gun...

"Give it to me..." she said...

"Oh I intend too..." Sean breathed...

"Give me the melatonin..." she said...

"I changed my mind..." Sean said as he stood up and picked up the gun...

"I don't understand..." Sonovia said...

"Flick – come have a drink..." Sean said. Flick got up and went over to his wife... "Take a glass of champagne..." Flick did as he was told... "Pick up a glass..." Sean said as he turned to Sonovia. She did as she was told... "Here's to us..." Sean said as he picked up a glass and took a sip...

"To us..." they said as they took a sip...

"Flick... since you like to watch... today's your lucky day..." he said as he put the bottle of melatonin back in the nightstand... "Drink up..."

"I'm not drinkin'..." Flick said...

"You're drinking..." Sean said as he put the gun in Sonovia's waist... "And so are you..." they both gulped down their champagne... "That's more like it..." he said and then he gulped down his glass... "Now – Flick – go sit in the chair – Snow – get on the bed..."

"Okay..." she said as she climbed on the bed, put her legs up under her chin, and put her arms in front of her...

Bazil was getting really annoyed as he sent another text, "What the hell is going on?! Why won't you answer me?!" Bazil looked at his phone for another minute or so and when he looked across the lobby he saw Aiden at the tables... "Fuck this!!" he said as he got up and went towards the elevator...

"Get on your back..." Sean commanded. Sonovia slid down next to him and lay on her back...

"That's better..." he breathed as he lay down beside her and bent down to kiss her...

"Get your ass up! Now!" Bazil boomed as he burst into the room...

"Bazil – I was..."

"Shut the fuck up!" Bazil growled as he bust him upside the head with the butt of his gun. Flick and Snow looked back and forth between the two of them... "Where's the money?"

"Right there..." Sean answered as he pointed to the duffel bags...

"Take the money..." Bazil commanded. Sean did as he was told... "Let's go..." Bazil commanded as he left the room and Sean followed. Flick jumped up and ran over to Sonovia...

"Flick... Oh God..." she cried...

"Baby... I'm sorry..." he cried...

"It wasn't your fault..."

"He's right – I should 'a killed him..."

"Just hold me Flick..."

"I gotchu..."

"I wanna take this off..."

"Okay..."

"I wanna burn it!"

"Okay..." Flick let go of her and she went into the bathroom...

"Hurry up!" Bazil demanded. Sean followed Bazil as he got closer to Aiden. Aiden was at the tables so Bazil kept a good distance...

"How am I gonna get his attention?" Sean asked...

144

"Tell him to meet you in the bathroom..."

"Okay..." Sean said as he went over to the tables...

"Hello Sean..." Aiden said...

"I need to go to the men's room – I'll be right back..." Sean said as he headed towards the men's room. Bazil waited for Aiden to follow Sean and then he followed them both...

"Sonovia?"

"Yea..."

"Can I come in?"

"Yea..." Flick went into the bathroom and saw the lingerie burning in the garbage...

"Baby... I'm sorry..." he whispered as he pulled her into a hug and started to cry...

"Uh uh Flick – stop that – we need to get the fuck outta here!"

"You right – c'mon..." Flick said as he took her by the hand and led her out to the bedroom... "Get that melatonin outta there..." he said as he pointed to the nightstand, opened the duffel bag... and bust out laughing...

"What the fuck you laughing at?!' Sonovia exclaimed...

"He took the wrong bag!" Flick laughed...

"What?!"

"Look! He took the wrong bag!" Flick laughed...

"Oh shit!" Sonovia laughed...

"Let's hurry up and get the fuck outta here!" Flick exclaimed...

"Is that my money?" Aiden asked...

"That's your money..." Sean answered. Bazil was listening outside the door...

"Are you in line?" Someone asked as they walked up...

"Yea..."

"I thought the ladies room was the only room that got lines..." the man laughed as he walked away. Bazil continued to listen...

"Is this a fucking joke?!" Aiden exclaimed...

"Oh shit – I grabbed the wrong bag – I'll get it..."

"Time's up..." Aiden said as he grabbed Sean by his head with both hands and snapped his neck. Bazil fought back tears as he heard Sean's body hit the floor... "Stupid mutha fucka!!" Aiden exclaimed. Bazil moved out the way as Aiden came out the bathroom and Bazil watched him go back to the tables. Once Bazil knew he was settled, he went back to the lobby of the hotel, got in the elevator, and headed back to Flick and Sonovia's room...